The Carpenter
And
Other Stories

Retold by Susan Price

THE CARPENTER AND OTHER STORIES

SUSAN PRICE

1

CONTENTS

2

CONTENTS

1

The Wise Man in the Stone
And Thorhall's Vision

There once lived a man named Kodran, who had worshipped the old gods, Freyr and Freyja, Thor and Odin, all his life, as all his family before him had done; but during Kodran's lifetime the new faith of Christianity came to his country and his son became converted to it.

Kodran made no objections but took an interest in the faith and in the bishop who preached it. After a while he was heard to say that he was impressed by the devotion of the Christians to their god and that, in his opinion, their bishop had the second sight because he gave his followers such good advice. He might have gone to the bishop for advice himself, Kodran said, except that on his land was a great stone in which lived a wise man. The wise man in the

stone gave Kodran all the advice he needed, besides
guarding his cattle, predicting the weather and foretelling
the future.

What Kodran said was repeated from one to
another until the Christian bishop came to hear of it and
he was not pleased to learn of the wise man in the stone.
He was still less pleased when he heard of the fine scarlet
cloth and rich gold ornaments the wise man wore. The
bishop took prayer books, prayer-beads and holy water
and he walked over to Kodran's farm. When he found the
great stone, he prayed over it and sang psalms and
sprinkled it with holy water. He meant to drive out the
wise man.

That night, as Kodran slept in his bed, he thought
he saw the wise man from the stone standing beside him,
dressed in red and wearing gold finger-rings with another
ring of gold round his neck. The wise man's face was
swollen with weariness.

"Kodran," the wise man said, "why are you allowing
this stranger to treat me like this? He has banged on my
walls, he has howled and screeched all day long and he has
poured boiling water over my house until my children
cried out in pain. Make him go away, Kodran, and let us
have peace."

Kodran woke then and sat up quickly in bed, but the
wise man vanished the very second Kodran's eyes opened.
He saw nothing but the blurred shapes of his furniture in
the darkness and heard no voice, but only the fire burning
low and ashes falling.

Kodran sat awake for a while, thinking over his
dream but although he knew the Christian bishop was on
his land, praying over the stone, he did not like to say
anything about it because his son was now a Christian.
Besides, he thought that the bishop would soon grow tired
of his praying and chanting.

But the bishop went on praying and, the next
night, Kodran dreamed of the wise man again. He had

taken off his golden ornaments and his scarlet clothes were crumpled and stained. "Kodran, Kodran," he said, "when will this hammering, this shrieking, this torture of scalding water, be over? This man would drive me from my home. I have always been helpful to you, Kodran: when will you make him stop? Make him go away, and let us have peace."

At day-break, Kodran remembered the dream but he still did nothing. He told himself that if the bishop did not stop this praying and hymn-singing soon, he would tell him to leave his land.

That night, the wise man came again. Now he wore a cloak of hard, black skin. His face was pale and ill.

"Kodran," he said, "we must go out from our stone, my family and I, and where shall we find another home now, with so many churches in the land, with so much hymn-singing and bell-ringing? I fear that when we are tired and need to rest, we will be driven on. When we are hungry and need to eat, we will be chased away. When we are cold and need to warm ourselves, there will be no fire we are allowed near. And so, we will wander always from place to place, homeless, betrayed by our protector, Kodran, and with no salvation at our lives' ends. I wish sorrow on you, Kodran, who would not help me when I asked, even though I have always given you good advice and guarded your house and your goods. You never knew bad luck or hard times while I worked for you, but since this is my reward, you will never receive such service again as I gave you." And the wise man lifted his cloak of black skin across his face. Kodran woke from the dream to find his farmhouse dark, empty and silent.

He never saw the wise man from the stone again, but he often remembered his last words because from that night, Kodran had no luck. His servants stole from him and were so careless of his property that he lost many cattle and sheep through disease. His sons quarrelled with him over his wealth and made his life miserable. But, as his wealth and hopes dwindled away, he became a Christian and so gained life eternal.

It is also said that a man with second sight lived in Iceland, at the time Christianity was first brought there. His name was Thorhall. One day he was found standing outside his farmhouse, staring at the country round about. He stood there a long time. When darkness was near, one of his sons asked him what the matter was. Thorhall shook his head sadly, but would not answer.

Some days later he was asked again what he had been staring at and why he'd looked so unhappy. He said, "I saw the hills opening and I saw all the people of the hills gathering together their pots and pans and other belongings. They packed them into sacks and all the time they were crying. When they had all their things on their backs and no more reason to stay, they came out from the hills, all of them, a great stream of them, and their journey brought them towards me. They were so many and the noise of their feet treading the ground was so constant and so loud, and their wailing and calling out of farewells to the places they loved so loud and so pitiful that I cannot understand why every man, woman and child in Iceland did not see and hear them. They passed close to me and I called out, asking them where they were going. 'Christ has come to Iceland,' one said to me, 'and we must leave. We must hurry away from the churches before they set the bells clanging, before the people begin praying and screeching hymns. We must go far away, Thorhall, friend, and we can never return.' Then they passed me by and went on all the long line of them, all the people of the hills. I watched them go and it came to me that no one after me would ever see a sight such as that I watched, that stories would be told of this and it would be disbelieved. That is why I am sad. We have gained Christ, but what have we lost?"

2

The Carpenter

S t. Cuthman wished to do God's will by building a church, one of the first in the land.

He knew that the building of a church was a serious business, not to be undertaken without forethought and prayer. Nothing about it could be done carelessly, not the digging of the postholes, not the cutting of the timber, nor the choosing of the site.

The choosing of the site was, perhaps, most important of all, for the place had to be one blessed by the Lord. The heathens had allowed their devil-gods to choose where a new house or temple would be built and it seemed right to St. Cuthman to let the One True God choose the site of His new house of worship.

There was much country to choose from, so St. Cuthman decided to travel from one place to another, never resting, until his God gave him some sign that he had reached the place where the church should be built.

St. Cuthman's plans were hindered by his mother, an ancient woman whose teeth had all worn down to her gums long before and whose watering eyes were like clouded glass. St. Cuthman looked at her as she sat by the fire, licking her gums and dabbing at her eyes and he knew that he could not leave her behind— yet nor could he let her keep him from his duty. That night he prayed for advice; and the next morning he wrapped his mother up well, loaded her into a wheelbarrow and began his long journey.

He pushed his mother, in the wheelbarrow, from Devon to Sussex and over all that distance, in all that time, Cuthman was sent no sign from God that any of the places they passed were suitable for a church. But, as he neared the town of Steyning, the wheelbarrow broke and let his poor old mother fall on to the ground with a crash and a squeal. Some men were making hay in a field nearby and they saw it all— the bony, lanky man struggling to push along the little old lady bundled into the barrow, and then the shock, the legs in the air and the shouting. All the haymakers laughed, setting down their tools so they could laugh harder, and point and jeer.

St. Cuthman was angry. "Laugh man," he shouted, "but weep, Heaven." Immediately rain poured down on that one field, hard rain that broke down the standing grass and drenched what had been cut. At the exact borders of the field, on each of its sides, the downpour stopped— and the haymakers stopped laughing. They gaped as they saw all their work spoiled. They called out to St. Cuthman, begging him to forgive them and take away his spell.

Too late. St. Cuthman had mended his barrow with withies from the hedge and pushed his mother away along the road.

After only a short walk, the barrow broke again and dropped his old mother into the wet grass. Then St. Cuthman saw that this was his sign. Here was where he was meant to stop and build his church. At once he started work and cut branches to make a small shelter where he and his mother could live while the church was made. That night, inside their shelter, they ate and prayed. The next day, St. Cuthman started work on his church.

He cut the timber and cleared the ground and levelled it, which was all hard work. He marked out the ground-plan and dug the postholes. It was tiring but all went well until it came to the fitting together of the timbers. Cuthman had no skill at carpentry. He had not the right tools and when he begged or borrowed the right tools, he didn't know how to use them. Saws would not cut straight for him. Hammers, in his hands, hit nothing but his thumbs; and whatever he measured either stretched or shrank when he turned his back and would not fit together. Weeks passed and still the church was nothing but a pattern of postholes in the ground.

Then, striding along the road, came a man with a bag of tools on his back. He stopped to watch the Saint's fretful work and St. Cuthman scowled at him. The stranger was neither young nor old and, though he wasn't very tall, he looked strong, as if he was used to walking for long distances and working with his hands and arms and back. Long dark hair hung over his shoulders and mixed with his black beard. "What are you doing?" he asked the Saint.

"I am trying to build a church," said the Saint and sweated with embarrassment under the stranger's stare and grew clumsy and dropped things.

The stranger left the road and wandered among the pieces, large and small, of discarded timber. He said, "What you need is a carpenter."

"I don't have a carpenter," said the Saint. "I have one old mother and she is worse at woodwork than I am."

"I'm a carpenter," said the stranger. He jerked his thumb over his shoulder at the bag on his back. "I have all my tools here."

St. Cuthman stared at him. "What do you want in exchange for staying here and working on my church?"

The carpenter smiled. "Oh, let's get it finished before we talk of that." He dropped the bag of tools from his shoulder and took off his coat.

That day, and for many days after, Cuthman ran about at the orders of the carpenter, even though he was a saint. He was almost happy to do it, for this carpenter was a master of his craft. Every one of his tools had been worn to the grasp of his hand and, once in his hand, they seemed to move of their own accord, he used so little effort. Cuthman's hands were soft and blistered, but the carpenter's palms and fingers were protected by thick callouses.

The carpenter stroked every piece of wood with loving attention, as if trying to remember every detail of its texture, grain and scent. He would fit it to its brother-beam and they would fit as close as if they'd grown together. The wallposts were sunk, the planks for the walls were fixed together with pegs of wood, the roof-beams were raised; and through all the hard work, the carpenter smiled and often sang or whistled. He darted about so quickly that St. Cuthman couldn't keep up with him as he followed with the bag of tools.

The Saint didn't like the carpenter's singing and smiling. "Can't you be quiet? We're about God's work. It should be done in prayerful silence."

"Oh, why should God mind a little whistling?" the carpenter said. "I can't help myself. I love the wood! I love the work!"

St. Cuthman tut-tutted, and frowned whenever he heard some dance-tune being hummed— but he was afraid to say too much in case the carpenter was offended and went away before the church was finished.

At last, it was finished: every shingle was in place on the roof; the little wooden door swung on leather hinges; and above the door was a wooden cross. The two men, the carpenter and the Saint, stood looking at it. Both sighed with satisfaction.

"Now, my dear good fellow," said the Saint. "You must tell me how I can pay you. Shall I spend my life in praying for your soul? Is there some sin of which you wish to be absolved? Is there any advice I can give you, or some theological difficulty which I can explain so you can understand your God better?"

The carpenter smiled, picked up his bag of tools and swung them to his shoulder. "No, Cuthman," he said. "But keep my laws." And he vanished.

Of all the early saints, none was more humble than St. Cuthman.

3

The Priest and the Neckan

There was once a preacher who travelled from one town to another as he spread word of Christ. As he climbed a steep mountain track, he came upon a deep pool caught in a hollow. He heard music and looked round to see who played. He saw the spirit of the pool, a Neckan.

The Neckan sat above the pool on a rock. It looked like a handsome young man with long, wet hair. It played beautifully on a golden harp and sang in a strong, clear, pleasing voice.

Everything about the Neckan displeased the preacher. He was angry that it even existed. He hated that it was so beautiful and made such lovely music. He was even more angry that it seemed so happy as it sat idly there, doing nothing useful.

The preacher called out, "Why do you sing, Neckan?" He shook the long walking staff he carried.

"You should weep and mourn. You may live a thousand years but at the end you will die and there's no salvation for you! Into the dark you'll go and you'll be forgotten."

The Neckan broke off its music. It stared at the preacher and then cried out, "No salvation?"

"None!" said the preacher and struck his staff on the ground. "Why, this stick I hold here, withered and dead as it is, will bud and leaf before the day you shall be redeemed, you Godless thing!"

The Neckan gave a long cry and threw its harp into the deep pool, where it sank with one deep, water-drawn chord. With another cry, the Neckan threw itself from the rock after the harp and disappeared beneath the water.

The preacher laughed and climbed on up the mountain track. He was no longer angry, but felt strong and good because he had brought a creature of darkness to knowledge of its doom. Smiling, he turned his bearded face to catch the breeze and looked on the beautiful trees, flowers, sky and all that the good God had created.

But as he walked, he began to be bothered by a buzzing in his ears. No matter how he turned his head, the buzzing would not go away.

Bees were circling his head. He waved them away but they returned, more and more of them. Then, from the corner of one eye, he caught sight of his walking staff.

He stopped, held his staff out at arm's length and stared at it. Not only had the staff budded and leafed, it had budded and flowered. Its deep blue flowers released a heavy and beautiful scent— and from everywhere, bees and others insects came flying towards them.

The preacher stood very still on the mountainside, watching the bees struggle into the flowers and wondering at the miracle. He remembered the words he had spoken to the Neckan and he was deeply ashamed.

He turned and climbed back down the mountain path, followed by a stream of bees. He found the Neckan standing waist deep in its pool, sobbing into its hands.

"Neckan," said the preacher, gently. "Look." When the Neckan raised its head, the preacher held out the blossoming staff. "Neckan," said the preacher, "I was wrong. I am ashamed and I am sorry."

Quick as a fish, the Neckan dived beneath the water and rose again with its golden harp. It played, and sang about the flowers and leaves that could grow even from a dead staff. The preacher sat on the bank and listened, and watched the bees feeding on his miraculous, flowering staff.

4

St. Cullen and the Elves

St. Cullen did not like the company of others. Their behaviour distracted him from his thoughts on the goodness of God and so he searched for a lonely place, far from houses and paths, where he could make himself a hermitage.

He found the place he wanted at the foot of Glastonbury Tor. There he built himself a small hut from branches, rough stones, clay and turfs. It looked nothing like a place where someone lived and could easily have been mistaken for an overgrown mound.

Which it soon was. Two men came by one day and stopped to rest on the mound, without realizing that they were sitting almost in St. Cullen's doorway.

St. Cullen was inside his hut, trying to pray, but he overheard every word the men said. One man told the other that the King of the Elves had his palace on top of the Tor. He went on to describe the lovely ornaments, paintings and hangings to be found in the palace; the beautiful music to be heard there and the food and clothes of the Elves, which were far better than anything to be found among mortals.

St. Cullen tried not to listen. He went on kneeling in his hut, waiting for the men to go away. Instead, they went on and on talking about the fairies— their golden plates, their beautiful women, their perfumes, their silks— and every word made the saint angrier. At last, he couldn't stand it any longer. He stuck his head out of his hut and shouted, "Go away! Or, if you will not do that, then be quiet! I cannot be hearing any more of this chatter about devils."

The two men jumped to their feet in a fright and looked about everywhere. It seemed to them that the ground had suddenly yelled at them. Eventually they spotted the saint's angry face peering out of what they'd taken for a mound of stones and old trees. "Go away yourself," said one of the men. "We weren't talking about devils and the Elf King will be insulted that you call him by such a name."

"The creatures of which you spoke are not God's, and therefore they are devils," said the Saint. "Go away! And don't argue with me— I'm a Saint."

The two men gathered up their belongings and started to leave. One turned back and said, "Well, then, Saint, you'll be sorry for those words. The King of the Elves will send for you, you'll see."

The Saint didn't think so and was happy enough to be rid of the two men. But the next day, in the evening, a stranger came to the Saint's cell. He was a small man, very dark of hair and eye, and dressed in red. He said, "My master, the King, is in his palace on the hill-top and is waiting to receive you, Cullen, if it would please you to come."

St. Cullen put his head out of the hut and looked

up at the hill-top. "I see no palace," he said. "Don't bother me with your nonsense."

The stranger bowed and said, politely, that he would trouble Cullen no more that night, but would return the following night. Then he went away.

Early the next evening the stranger returned and begged St. Cullen to go with him to the King's palace. The King was anxious to meet him.

"Where is this palace?" Cullen demanded.

The stranger pointed towards the top of the hill. "There."

The Saint stepped from his cell and looked up. He saw no building of any kind, neither large nor small. In silence, he turned his back on the stranger and returned to his cell.

"I will trouble you no more tonight," said the stranger, "but I shall return tomorrow, and the next night, and the next, and so on, until you agree, for my King is determined to meet you."

The stranger did indeed return, night after night, until St. Cullen saw that he was not going to give up. So, the Saint filled a bottle with stream water and blessed it, to make it holy. The next evening, when the stranger came, the Saint agreed to go with him. He took the bottle of holy water with him, hidden under his cloak.

He followed the small, dark man to the top of the hill and only when they were at the top did he see the palace. It was full of light, which poured from a great many windows and doors. The air was full of the sound of lovely music and the smell of delicious food.

The messenger led the Saint into a room of dazzling light. Round the walls hung tapestries in rich, bright colours and at the centre of the room was a long table loaded to the point of collapse with food. Hot meats sizzled in their grease, warm cakes released a scent of spice and fruit, and there was a warm smell of ale boiled with honey. The Saint was not used to eating much food— and the little he did eat was very plain— so the sight and smell of so much almost overpowered him.

The Elves crowded close about him, curious to see and touch him. He disliked their jostling. Light flashed from their jewels as sunlight flashes from a mirror. It sparkled from their golden chains and ornaments and also from their hard eyes.

The crowd parted to let through the Elf King, wearing his golden circlet and attended by many little pages, all dressed in red and blue livery. "You are welcome, Cullen," said the King. "I have waited a long time to meet you. I hear that you think us devils but tell me, have you ever heard of such splendour as this amongst the miseries of Hell?"

Cullen looked about the Elf palace. "I think little of a hillside cave, muddy, filthy and running with water," he said, and at once the glamour was destroyed. The wet and dirty walls showed through the hangings, and the smell of wet earth smothered the smell of food.

The King quickly led the Saint to the table, and invited him to eat as much as he liked, so they might be friends, since they were already neighbours.

St. Cullen looked at the food with distaste. "I do not eat the dried and shrivelled leaves from a tree." At once the hot meats, cakes and fruits were seen for what they really were.

Still, the Elves could not believe that the Saint could see through their glamour. The King said, "How do you like my pages? Do I not have more than any other king? Is not their livery of scarlet and blue fine?"

"It is apt," said Cullen. "Blue for the eternal cold and red for the eternal flames, of Hell— and Hell is your proper place." He took the bottle of holy water from under his cloak and threw it over them all. The music stopped on the instant, leaving only a dull silence. The walls, the tables, the courtiers, all vanished. There was not even a cave. St. Cullen stood in the cold air on the open hillside, with grass beneath his feet and a dark sky over his head.

He climbed backdown the hill, went into his cell, prayed and went to bed.

The Elves were never seen in that country again.

5

The Bogey

There was once a bogey who haunted a river pool. He was rarely seen while it was light but still, few people would go near that pool by night or day. It was known as the Old Bogey Hole and it belonged to a rich farmer who owned a great deal of the land in that part of the country.

The bogey used to work for the farmer and in return he was given milk and bread, which was left for him on the farmhouse doorstep every night. The bogey kept the yards, barns, stables and byres tidy and was also a good hand at mowing, stooking and threshing, so he earned his keep and the farmer was careful to do nothing that might offend him.

The farmer's daughter saw the bogey often. She'd been taught since childhood to think of him as a friend and was not afraid of him. She would often walk by the Old Bogey Hole and no harm ever came to her. It was said that she was under the bogey's protection.

People were even more sure of this when it was announced that the girl was to be married. In the middle of the night, a bale of white silk was thrown at the farmhouse door with a thump and fell onto the step. Who but the bogey could have provided it? And in such a manner?

The girl's wedding dress was made from the silk and she did not forget the bogey. On her wedding night, his bowl was filled with ale instead of milk and his bread was replaced with cake. All that night he sang drunkenly about the farmhouse in the darkness.

The new husband came to live in his wife's house and helped his father-in-law with the farm-work. Within a year, gossip said that the new wife was expecting a baby— and then, after the months had passed by, it was time for her to have it. It was in the Autumn and the young woman's first labour pains began in the middle of a nasty night: dark, windy and pouring with rain.

Her husband ran out into the yard to wake the stable-lad, shouting at him to ride as fast as he could to fetch the midwife, while the girl's mother and father shouted from their bedroom window that the boy was to ride by the quickest way— right past the Old Bogey Hole.

The stable-lad dressed, but very slowly. He wished no harm to his master's daughter but he didn't want to go near the Old Bogey Hole. The more slowly he pulled on his shirt and fastened his buttons, the longer it would be before he had to risk meeting the bogey.

The stable-lad didn't know it, but the bogey was a few feet from him, at work in the stable-yard. The bogey heard all the shouting and knew what was happening. He saw the stable-lad taking his time and he knew why.

The bogey opened the farmhouse door and took a cloak from behind it. He led out and mounted the best horse in the stable— he needed no tack or saddle— and rode off to fetch the midwife at a full gallop. That horse had never run faster and never would again. It ran as if it had a bogey on its back.

The bogey reached the midwife's house and hammered at the door and shutters, yelling out that she was needed and must come quick. She came hurrying out as soon as she could and saw a man, tightly wrapped in a cloak, waiting on a horse. She allowed him to help her up onto the horse— but then the horse lunged away at such speed that she squealed and flung her arms tightly around the man in front of her. She had been fetched in a hurry a few times but had never been rattled along, on a saddleless horse, at such a fierce pace, nor had to hold on so tightly. Then she realized they were taking the road to the Old Bogey Hole.

"Oh, not this way," she cried. "We might meet the bogey and I'm scared."

"Never mind, old girl," said the horse's rider. "You've met all the bogeys you're going to meet tonight." She was a little comforted.

They rushed through the pool, throwing up water on all sides, and were at the farm in so short a time that the stable-lad was only just pulling on his boots. While the midwife hurried into the house, the bogey dragged the boy into the yard and beat him all around the barn and byre, saying, "That's for not taking better care of the young missis."

The farmer's daughter had a baby girl and when the stable-lad told him about the bogey's ride and who had really fetched the midwife, the farmer was as proud of his bogey as he was of his daughter and granddaughter. He told the tale to everyone he met. He even told it to the priest, who said that such a good servant should be baptized. The farmer wasn't sure about this but didn't like to argue with the priest.

The priest invited himself to stay at the farm and arrived with a large flask of holy water. At dinner, he asked many questions about the bogey's comings and goings.

Then he went out into the stable and waited.

Some time after midnight, the bogey came in, to see if the place needed tidying. The priest raised the flask of holy water high and poured the water all over him.

The bogey shrieked in pain and anger, flailing his arms as he tried to rid himself of the scalding water drops. He ran out into the yard, howling, and the priest ran after him— but the bogey vanished into the dark.

After that, the bogey did no more work for the farmer and wasn't seen for many years. Some said that the priest's holy water had sent him to Hell. Others thought he'd only gone away to haunt some other part of the country. But most thought the bogey was still somewhere near the Old Bogey Hole and stayed away from it. And they were right.

It was the farmer who saw the last of the bogey. Late one spring evening he was leading his plough-team home. As he passed the pool, the bogey jumped up in his way and said, "Give us a lend of your horses, man."

The farmer was startled and took a moment to catch his breath. Then he thought that he didn't want to lend his horses to a creature that wasn't even human. "What do you want with my horses?"

"I need 'em," said the bogey. "Since they built that new church just down the hill, my old woman and my childer can't get any rest for them blasted ding-dongs they strung up in the tower. So, lend us your horses, man, to help us move out of hearing of 'em. I always helped you before. And how is the young lass and the little lass?"

"They're very well," said the farmer. "Thanks to you." He handed the leading reins of his horses to the bogey and went on home without looking back. He spent an anxious evening and night waiting for his horses' return but when they trotted into the yard the next morning, they had glossier coats and a more dancing step that he'd seen in them for years. They looked like two-year olds and worked like them too, so the bogey more than paid for the loan of them. But where the bogey had moved his family was never discovered— and the horses weren't telling. It must have been well out of earshot of the new church's bells, since he was never again seen in that district. People even stopped speaking of his old pool as haunted.

6

King Olaf's Warning

One of the first Christian kings of Norway was Olaf Tryggvason. He was feared because of the magical protection and powers of foresight which his new faith gave him— and because, if his countrymen refused to give up the worship of their old Gods, he killed or maimed them.

This meant that the King's words were listened to when he announced that he had been sent a vision. The vision had told him that it would be dangerous for any man to go outside alone that night. If any man needed the privy, he must waken a friend to go with him. All the soldiers and servants who slept in the King's hall promised to do this.

Much, much later, when it was dark and the hall's fires had burned low, when everyone had been asleep for a long time, a man named Thorstein woke. He had eaten and drunk a lot before lying down and now he was in great discomfort and had a strong need for the privy. He kicked off his blanket and scrambled to his feet— and remembered the King's warning and the promise he had made.

Thorstein tried to wake one of his friends, but it was as if some spell of dullness lay over the sleepers in the hall. They muttered and turned but they would none of them wake. Thorstein's need for the privy grew more and more urgent until, at last, he had to dash out of the hall as fast as he could, no matter what the King had said.

The Royal Privy was a magnificent building, with strong walls and a high roof. Inside, there were eleven seats at each of the longer walls, so that twenty-two of the courtiers or garrison could ease themselves at one, in comfort and good company.

Thorstein hurried into the privy, unfastening his trousers as he entered, and dropped himself down over the hole nearest to the door. He thought being close to the door meant that he could run back to the safety of the hall quickly, if there were any danger. As his bare bottom touched the wood of the seat, he felt, on that side of him furthest from the door, a cold draught and a breath of heat.

A stink of sulphur and ashes crept to his nose and all the hairs of his head, beard and body stirred. Looking from the corner of his eyes, he thought he saw something move, so he fractionally turned his head— and cried out in terror as he saw, rising from the furthest privy, a creature more hideous than his own nightmares or any artist's carving had ever shown him.

The creature rose completely from the privy and appeared to sit on it. Turning its frightful head, it looked at Thorstein. There were nine empty seats between them. "It's a good night, Thorstein," the creature said.

In fear and horror, Thorstein cried out, "What are you?"

"I am one of those old heroes, Thorstein, who, in ancient times, fought with the great Harald War-Tooth of Denmark. You will have heard tell of us, surely?"

"But Harald War-Tooth is long dead," Thorstein said. "How are you come here?"

"I am long dead too," said the creature, "and I am come up from Hell. In my day we had not heard of your King's Christ, and we are all damned."

"Come up from Hell?" cried Thorstein. "Why? Why have you come?"

The creature gaped and grinned and said, "For you, Thorstein."

Thorstein tried to jump up from his seat, to run back to the hall, but found that he was fixed in his place, gripped by the same spell of dullness and weakness that had prevented him from waking his friends. Looking again at the thing, he saw it preparing to move towards him. He knew then that he would have to talk, and talk, for his life and soul. Such a creature as he was faced with had to answer any question put to it, so as long as he could keep it talking, he was safe.

"You come from Hell," he said. "Then tell me—I've often wondered— of all the damned, who bears the pains of Hell most bravely and with least outcry?"

The creature sank back onto its seat. "That would be Sigurd the Volsung, who slew the dragon and bathed in its blood."

"And what torture does he endure?" Thorstein asked hastily, as soon as the thing had finished speaking.

"He kindles an oven," said the creature.

"What? Kindles an oven? No wonder he bears it bravely. That's no very terrible torture."

"No?" said the creature. "I don't think you would bear it so bravely, Thorstein. The kindling Sigurd uses is himself."

Thorstein was so astonished at this that he fell silent and almost didn't notice when the creature moved

31

again. But he recovered in time and called out, "Who bears the pains of Hell least bravely and with most outcry?"

The thing sank back onto its seat again. "That would be Starkad the Old, even though in life he was among the most courageous of Odin's warriors."

"What is his torture?"

"He lies with his ankles in the fire."

"His ankles in the fire? And he one of Odin's most courageous warriors? Surely a truly brave man would bear that with more fortitude?"

"I don't think you would," said the creature. "His ankles are in the fire, true, but only the soles of his feet are out of it. And he yells, Thorstein, oh, how he yells. Would you like to hear how loudly he yells?"

Before Thorstein could reply, the thing opened its mouth and gave such a shriek that the sound struck Thorstein like a blow to the head and caused darkness to pass before his eyes as if he had blinked. With horrible speed, during that blink of darkness, the creature moved three seats closer to him and said, "That is how Starkad yells when his pain is least. When it is greater, *this* is how he screams."

Thorstein again tried to speak but before he could, the creature screamed, even more loudly and roughly. The sound tore at Thorstein's head. Darkness came again but for a longer time. When he could see once more, the thing was only three seats from him, grinning and gloating and saying, "But this is how Starkad shrieks when his pain is at its worst."

Thorstein knew that this time he would lose his senses completely and the thing would reach him and carry him down to Hell— but as the thing screeched and as Thorstein, still fixed to his seat, fell back in a dead faint, the bell of the King's chapel jangled, ringing loudly through the darkness and murk of the demon's spell. With a groan, the demon sank down through the seat it was then sitting on, and friends rushed into the privy to lift

Thorstein up from the floor where he had fallen as the spell broke.

He was helped back to the hall where the chapel bell still rang and where the King waited to see if Thorstein had been saved. The King had been uneasy about his vision and had risen in the night to make sure that all were safe. Missing Thorstein from his sleeping place, the King had ordered the chapel bell to be rung immediately.

Thorstein was so grateful to the King for saving his life that he became one of his most faithful followers and so shaken was he by his terrible experience in the Royal Privy that it was said he became one of the most pious and devoted Christians in the whole of Norway.

.

7

Merlin

There was once a boy whose mother was a nun but whose father was a devil.

As soon as the nun told of the devil's visits to her, priests were sent for and they made the sign of the cross over her and sprinkled her with holy water and gave her holy water to drink. Because of all this, when the child was born, he seemed to be a normal human child. He was named Merlin and, as soon as he could leave his mother, he was taken away to a monastery, to be raised by monks.

There he was taught to read and write and proved to be a very clever boy. But no matter how the monks tried, they could not make him pious. He would not attend chapel, nor pray, not cross himself. All these things made him itch, he said.

He had other talents besides reading, which made the monks fear him. He could heal wounds and sickness, read minds, foresee the future and look into the past. The monks thought this the result of the devil's blood in him and they beat him many times, to drive the devil out. Strangely, the beatings did not make Merlin like Christianity any better and while he was still a small boy, he ran away from the monastery.

The monks often worried about what they had let loose on the world, and prayed for Merlin's soul, if he had one. For many long years, they heard no news of him.

In the land to the far north of the monastery, the people were wild and savage heathens, ruled over by a pagan, King Gwentholeu. Word came to the monastery from this distant land that the wicked King had a new poet at his court. This poet was not only skilled in making verses, but in healing the sick and foretelling the future. His name was Merlin. Although still only a boy, this Merlin had won the favour of King Gwentholeu and went about dressed as finely as the King himself, with a bejewelled golden ring around his neck.

A story was told of this Merlin's most famous prophecy and it filled the monks with wonder and dread. Soon after Merlin had arrived at King Gwentholeu's court, a newborn baby boy had been brought to him and the parents had asked for the child's fortune to be told.

Merlin, it was said, told the parents to prepare themselves for sorrow: the child would not live long.

The parents were shocked. "Can you tell me how my son will die?" the father asked.

"By falling from a cliff," Merlin has said.

The parents went away but were much grieved and soon after, the child's uncle came and asked how his nephew would die, hoping he might hear a better answer.

"By hanging," Merlin said.

The uncle went away, bewildered; and soon after the child's grandfather came and asked, "How will my grandson die?"

"By drowning," Merlin said.

Now people began to laugh at Merlin behind his back. What kind of prophet foretold three different deaths for one small child? No, they said: this Merlin might be a good enough poet but he was no seer.

Merlin let them think what they pleased. A little more than a year later they had to think again. The baby was then grown to a toddler and, like all small children then, wore a long gown.

Escaping from its mother one day, it toddled and crawled off on an adventure, which brought it to a stream with steep banks. Stumbling, it fell over the bank and its long gown was tangled in a thorn bush. There it dangled from the bush, with its head in the water. When found, it was dead.

The child had died by falling from a cliff, by hanging and by drowning.

No one doubted Merlin's prophecies after that.

Merlin grew to be a young man no different in appearance from other young men, except that he was extraordinarily hairy. He remained King Gwentholeu's favourite poet but, year by year, Christianity had spread from the south until even the neighbouring kingdom of Strathclyde had become Christian.

Strathclyde was ruled by King Rytherch and at King Rytherch's court there was a Christian holy man named Kentigern, who was a saint.

Saint Kentigern was eager to convert every living soul to his Christian faith and day after day, he urged King Rytherch to make war on all those kingdoms which were still pagan. Since they would not listen to peaceful preaching, they must be forced to accept the Way and the Light by the sword. So said Saint Kentigern.

King Gwentholeu and the rulers of the other pagan kingdoms learned of this, and they began storing arrows and spears, ready to defend themselves.

Merlin went to King Gwentholeu and said, "Do

not sit at ease on your throne, waiting for Rytherch to come with his army. Attack him first! Drive back these Christians. You and your people have worshipped your gods since the beginning of time— will you give them up because this Kentigern says you must? Treat the Christians as they would treat you. Make war on them, destroy them, drive them from our land Your name will then be remembered, with love, by all those who worship our gods for hundreds of years to come."

Things fell out as both Merlin and Kentigern wished: a Christian and a Pagan army met. A battle was fought. Kentigern urged his army to fight for the salvation of their souls, for new glory, for God's city on earth.

Merlin beseeched his army to fight for the gods of their fathers, for ancient glory, for all their old and well-loved ways, for their sacred groves and streams and stone circles.

Then both joined their armies, Kentigern in his grey robe, a club in his hand and a wooden cross about his neck; Merlin in his brightly coloured clothes of expensive cloth, a golden ring about his neck and a sword as his weapon.

The battle was hard fought for a whole day and, at the end, the Christians won. Merlin's King, Gwentholeu, was killed. The pagans were chased from the field and Merlin found himself among the corpses of men he had persuaded to fight a battle fated to be lost. In his heart, he had known it must be lost, but his hatred of the new faith was so strong that he, the famous prophet, had hidden that knowledge from himself.

Merlin wept and as he wept, a loud voice cried out, "Merlin, devil's child! See what slaughter you have caused! You have chosen the devil's side and since your very nature is diabolical, you shall live with brutes until the day of your death."

Looking up, Merlin was dazzled by the enormous figure of a shining angel. Terrified, he ran away. He lost his wits and went deep into the forest, wandering there for many years. Thorns ripped his clothes from him and only his natural hairiness kept him warm in the winter. For year after year, he heard only the talk of birds and animals, and he lost the power of human speech. He lived on leaves and roots, berries, nuts, raw eggs and raw meat, like an animal.

During all this time Saint Kentigern had been travelling around the newly conquered pagan kingdoms, preaching the words of Christ. One day as he walked through the hills, he saw a large, hairy creature watching him from the thick undergrowth beside the track. The Saint stopped and stared at the thing. He saw that it was a man, but a naked, hairy, filthy, wild man.

The Saint sat down beside the track and began speaking gently to the strange creature. He did not stare at it, but looked at the ground and held out his hand while saying, "There is no need to be afraid. No harm shall come to you. Are you hungry?"

After a long time, with much patience, the Saint coaxed the creature to leave the bushes and come close to him. The Saint gave the creature bread from his satchel, which it ate greedily. "Have you heard of Jesus Christ?" the Saint asked. "Do you know that Christ loves you and will save you?"

The wild man cocked his head and seemed to listen— and then he said, "Merlin!" The power of speech returned to him and he eagerly told the Saint of how he had urged the pagans to fight against the Christians and how the loving Christian God had cursed him with madness and a life among the brutes.

"Do not despair," Kentigern said. "Our God is ever ready to forgive one who truly repents. He rejoices more over a sinner saved than over the salvation of righteous men. Repent, Merlin. Come to Christ."

But Merlin jumped up and ran away.

Kentigern knelt and prayed hard that God would lift the curse from Merlin, for in his present state he was little better than an animal. Once brought to live among other people, though, he might repent and come to Christ at last.

Merlin knew nothing of this, for he was wandering through the wilds, as mad as before. But then he came on a spring of fresh water where no water had been before. He drank from it and was calmed. His wits returned again. He looked down at himself and saw that he was naked and realized that he had been mad. He remembered talking with the Christian holy man and he made his way back to the track that crossed the mountains, searching for Kentigern.

The Saint was delighted to see him and gave him food and clothes. "Merlin, do you now wish to become a Christian?"

"I wish that I had not urged my King and his followers to fight against you," Merlin said, "because I see now that the coming of your faith was fated and I deluded myself in thinking that you could be beaten. But for myself, I still long for the times when there were many gods and goddesses and the people could worship what gods they chose."

"But they were unloving gods!" said Kentigern. "Come now, Merlin. Accept the body and the blood and become a Christian."

Merlin got to his feet and said, "I will no longer fight against you, for I see clearly now that it is no use. But neither will I break faith with my dead King and friends, with my gods and with my father. I will never accept your body and blood."

"I foresee a time when you will," said Kentigern.

"I doubt your powers of prophecy, Christian," Merlin said, "but now I will prophecy. I foresee that neither you, nor your King Rytherch, will live a day longer than I, for all the great power of your loving god."

Kentigern shook his head. "This is the power of the devil in you."

Merlin gave no answer, but left Kentigern and travelled the country as a poet and story-teller, often prophesying and always remaining faithful to his old gods and his father. At last, he came to the court of King Uther Pendragon, who admired Merlin's poetry so much that he made him his Court Poet, even though he knew Merlin was of demonic birth and a pagan. In a short while, Merlin became the King's most valued adviser, for even if his prophecies were devilish, they were useful. It was Merlin who foretold that King Uther would be killed shortly before the birth of his son and that the baby's life would be in great danger— but that if he survived, he would grow to be the greatest and most famous King that had ever reigned, or ever would reign, in Britain.

It was Merlin who, after King Uther's death, smuggled the baby away to place of safety; and it was Merlin who named him 'Arthur.'

From that time, Merlin worked to ensure that the boy would achieve the glorious reign he had foreseen for him. Merlin oversaw his education, devised a means for him to gain the throne despite his enemies, advised him after his coronation and provided him with his sword, Excalibur. He served the young King well and faithfully in everything even though Arthur, like his father, was a Christian.

Merlin himself never ceased to mourn for the passing of the old faith and it said that after he saw King Gwentholeu and the pagans defeated, he laughed only three more times in his life.

The first time was when he saw a husband and wife together, the husband tenderly patting his wife's hand and the wife smiling at him with loving kindness. But both of them had leaves in their hair and Merlin knew that they had both come straight from forest meetings with other lovers.

The second time he laughed was when he saw a ragged, starving beggar sitting by the roadside, for Merlin saw that the man sat directly above a hoard of gold and silver packed into a precious alabaster vase.

He laughed for the third time when he overheard a young man boasting of the new shoes he had just bought, which were so well made, of such fine leather, that they would last for seven years. Merlin knew that the young man would be dead before nightfall.

Merlin's life on this earth ended when he fell in love with a beautiful lady of Arthur's court, the lady Vivienne. Merlin knew very well that she did not love him, but he could not help but love her and followed her everywhere until people sneered and laughed at him whenever Arthur could not hear them.

Vivienne pretended to love Merlin in return until she had learned what seemed to her the greater part of his magic. Then, as they sat beneath an oak tree, she caused the tree's trunk to open and enclose Merlin, making him a prisoner at the oak's heart. She went away laughing.

Three days after this, one of Arthur's knights was riding by the tree when he heard Merlin calling from within it. Dismounting, the knight begged Merlin to tell him how to break the spell, but Merlin replied that it was not possible. He wanted the knight to carry a message to Arthur. He was to tell the young king what had happened, and warn him that, in the future he would have to rely on his own wisdom, because Merlin would no longer be able to advise him.

Then the knight heard Merlin call out to his father, the devil, asking for help and rescue. It was mid-day but the sun was suddenly covered and all became as black as midnight. In the darkness, the terrified knight heard a rushing sound and a rising gabble of unearthly voices. Merlin gave one last shout, which was heard three miles away and, at that moment, far away at Arthur's court in Camelot, the candles in the chapel were all blown out and the curtain behind Arthur's throne ripped from top to bottom.

An instant later the sky cleared. Daylight returned and the knight saw that the oak tree had been split, as if by lightening. Of Merlin there was no trace, nor has he ever been seen since.

8

The Knight's Servant

There was once a knight who lived in a castle high above an important road, along which anyone in that part of the country to wished to visit friends or relatives had to pass. So did anyone who wished to sell goods at market or trade in the towns on the other side of the mountains.

The knight watched their comings and goings from his castle and, whenever he saw a particularly rich party of travellers, he sent his men-at-arms down to rob them. Some of the travellers thought to save their lives and property by fighting but the knight's men always defeated them because they had more practice. They'd been robbing travellers for years.

Other travellers thought that if they gave up everything they had at once, they would be allowed to live but they too were mistaken. The knight had given orders that not a single person was to be allowed to escape or to live. Soon anyone still brave enough to travel by that road had to pass the wrecks of carts, discarded weapons, torn clothing, skeletons and even more horrible sights.

Strangely, though the knight was so cruel, he had a great love of the Virgin Mary. The chapel of his castle was dedicated to Her and every morning and every evening, and at midday, he knelt before the painting of Her which hung above the altar and asked Her to intervene for him with her Son. As a child he had been taught to pray to Her in this way and he had never forgotten. There was never a morning when he was so hungry that he did not go to the chapel first, and never an evening when he was tired that he went to be bed before kneeling to pray.

It happened that, one day, news was brought to the knight that a party of travellers had been sighted from the castle's tower. It was a large party with many horses and some rich, important person being carried in a litter. Even from the watch-towers the glittering and shining of necklaces, brooches and belts could be seen. The knight quickly decided that here was a party worth robbing and sent his men down to attend to the business.

All those men who were ready armed ran and jumped down the steep, dangerous path from the castle to the road and set about the travellers with such speed and brutality that, in a few minutes, every one of them was killed—except whoever was in the litter.

When the litter's curtains were ripped down, it was seen that a Bishop had been sitting behind them, dressed in silken robes, with a gold crucifix around his neck. At this the men drew back, being unwilling to kill a man of God in cold blood. Instead, they gathered up the weapons and purses of those they had killed.

The Bishop left his litter and came among them, asking them to take him with them back to the castle and to bring him before the knight who owned it. The men would not listen to him. They were afraid. Their arms full of stolen goods, they began their climb back to the castle's gates. The Bishop, though he was old, hoicked up his holy robes and followed them. He followed them right through the gates and into the castle, demanding to be taken to the knight.

No one wanted to be the one to tell the knight that the Bishop had been allowed to live and was inside his castle; but the Bishop cursed them in the name of God, insisting that they must take him to the knight. He had, he said, an important message for him. Then some of the men-at-arms were afraid and took the Bishop to the castle's hall, where the knight was sitting.

"Are you the master of this castle?" asked the Bishop. "Are you the man who has ordered the death of so many innocents, who had defied the commandments, 'Thou shalt not steal,' and 'Thou shalt not kill?'"

The knight grunted and said, "What are you doing here, old man? Who let you in?"

"I am here to give you a message from the only person you are ever likely to listen to— the Sainted Virgin Herself," said the Bishop. "But before I tell you what it is, you must have all of your servants called here so that I may see them."

"What are my servants to you?" demanded the knight.

"It is the Virgin's wish," said the Bishop.

The knight was angered but he would not deny a wish of the Virgin's— and who was more likely to know the Virgin's wishes than a Bishop? So, he sent for all his servants, telling them to come up to castle's great hall. They came and, as each of them entered, the Bishop called them to him and blessed them. Last of all, and very reluctantly, came the knight's personal servant, a small, stooping man. His job was to brush the knight's clothes, polish his boots and help him dress every morning and undress every night.

This small servant crept towards the Bishop a step

at a time, slowly and more slowly, until he stopped altogether while still at a distance from the holy man. The Bishop stretched out his hand to draw him closer but, to everyone's surprise, the little man began to twitch and squint. He chattered and pulled faces; he twisted his body and cringed down to the floor. Jumping up again, he arched over backwards until his head touched the floor behind him. He rolled up like a ball, he spun like a top, he bared all his teeth and opened wide his eyes. It was horrible to watch and it went on until the Bishop said, "You pitiable creature—unable to stand before a man of God. Now, in the name of the Holy Trinity, go back to your true place."

With a groan and sinking like a punctured balloon, the servant sank through the floor.

The knight, who had watched all this in horror, turned to the Bishop with his mouth open.

"You have been most cruel and wicked all your life," the Bishop said to him, "and you have never repented of your misdeeds. This creature, that you saw just now, was placed in your household by the Devil himself, that no time might be lost in carrying you to Hell. One thing and one thing only has been your salvation all these years, and that is your devotion to Our Lady, the Ever-Virgin. She has guarded you from harm, so that you might have a chance to repent; but I tell you, in Her name, that if you had even once forgotten the prayers you make to Her, in the mornings, the evenings and at midday, then that imp would have seized you with tooth and claw and snatched you away from your life. And now that you know how close you have been to eternal damnation, I beg you, confess and repent. Return to the Church."

The robber knight knelt, put his hands between those of the Bishop and confessed his sins, and repented, and swore to give up his wicked life of robbery and murder.

From that day, the road which ran below the

castle was safe for all travellers, for the knight never broke his vow. Indeed, to atone for all the sins he had committed, he went on a crusade to the Holy Land where, with the Church's blessing, he murdered many of the heathen and stole so much of their wealth that he was able to present the Bishop with a statue of the Virgin made of pure gold.

9

The Soldier and the Changeling

There was a soldier who returned home after many years of fighting abroad. His skin was burned to a dark brown, his hair was long and uncombed, and there hung round his waist, banging against his leg, a heavy, clumsy sword. On his back was fastened a bundle of his belongings and he hugged about himself an old cloak worn so thin that in places the colour of his shirt could be seen through it.

He had walked all day and now it was growing dark but the soldier trudged on. He was near the home he'd left many years before and thought that he might as well sleep under his family roof and save the price of lodgings. But the way was longer than he remembered and at near midnight, he was still walking. This is how he came to overhear the witches talking.

He was on one side of the hedge and they were on

the other and he heard one of them say, "A good morning to you, sister. Has it been a good night?"

"A good night, sister, a good night," replied the other. "I flew to the coast on the back of the miller's son— him being in the shape of a horse— and there I threw six cats, all tied together, into the sea and so raised a storm that will not be forgotten for a hundred years. But tell me, sister, has it been a good night for you?"

"It has been a good night, a good night indeed," said the first witch. "See what I have here." The soldier, listening, heard the witches exclaim with pleasure and wondered what it was they had. He crept closer to the hedge to try and see, but it was much too dark. Then one of the witches said, "Whose child is it?"

"Ah, that would be telling, sister. But it is a child that will be much missed, I promise you."

"And what did you leave in its place?" asked the other witch.

"One of the elves' children from under the hill: an ugly, screeching, nasty little thing. It will make the parents screech!"

The witches laughed, but the soldier now knew that they had a human baby, which they were going to give to the elves, and he knew that the elves would pay their tax to Hell with it, while the changeling had the best of everything and plagued the life out of the poor couple who believed it to be their child. The soldier drew his sword, and pushed right through the hedge, shouting, "In the name of Jesus Christ, give up that child!"

The witches were so alarmed that they at once changed into hares and sped away. The soldier caught the baby as it fell from where the witch's arms had been and used his cloak to wrap the child since, after pushing through the hedge there was hardly enough left to wrap around himself.

After that, he went on to his home and woke his mother and brothers and sisters by banging at the door.

They were all astonished to see him because for many years they had not known whether he was alive or dead. They were even more astonished to see him carrying a baby in his arms, but when they quietened down, he told them how he had rescued the child from the witches.

"Look after the baby, Mother," he said, giving it to her, "and very soon we shall hear who it belongs to. Then we'll be able to give it back."

Then, although his family wanted to fetch in all the neighbours to celebrate his return, the soldier went to bed. He was very tired.

Daylight came and, with it, a piece of gossip which was carried from door to door and eventually to the soldier's mother. Had she heard about all the fuss up at the big house? Did she know that the lord's little son had been stolen? The lord's son, fancy! Stolen away in the night and the nastiest, ugliest thing you wouldn't wish to meet left in its place.

"Fancy that, now," said the soldier's mother. She went straight inside to wake her son. As soon as he heard what she had to say, he said, "The lord's son, eh? If it had been anyone else, I'd have given them back the babby and been glad to do it. But since it's the lord, he can afford to pay us a little to make up for the common land he stole from us and all the trouble I had in the wars. 'Cos I'm sure he made a lot more from the fighting than I've come home with."

The soldier got up, wrapped the baby in his ragged old cloak so that it was quite hidden and walked over to the lord's house. He knocked at the door and when the lord answered, and asked what he wanted, the soldier said, "I'm a famous wizard and it's the luckiest day of your life. I've come to restore your son to you."

When he heard this, the lord immediately opened the door wide and let the soldier in. He led him up the stairs to the nursery, where the lord's wife was standing over the cradle, looking pale and scared. "Don't worry any more," said the soldier to her. "I am a wizard and I shall soon have your son back."

Going close to the cradle, the soldier looked inside and saw a creature no bigger than a baby but with the look of a tiny, shrivelled old man. It blinked at the soldier and curved its mouth in a thin, sly smile. Turning to the lord and lady, the soldier said, "I shall need an egg, a dish, a small spoon, a jug of water, a towel and some malt. The quicker you provide me with these things, the sooner you will see your son again."

The lord sent a servant running to fetch these things and while they waited, the lady said to the soldier, "Can you really bring back our son?"

"If you can," said the lord, "I'll give you anything you ask— anything. Land, money, cattle—"

"We'll talk about that later," said the soldier. "But I shall ask for the price my skill deserves, you may be sure of that."

Just then, the servant returned with the things he had asked for. The soldier carefully put his bundle, wrapped in his ragged old cloak, in a corner, and turned back to the lord and lady. Spreading his arms, he said, "Now I begin to weave my spell."

First, he moved the nursery table closer to the cradle, so the creature inside it could see everything he did.

Next, he broke the egg into the dish and washed out one half of the broken eggshell. He dried his hands carefully, one finger at a time.

The creature in the cradle took hold of the cradle's side with one bony hand and raised itself slightly, the better to see.

The soldier pretended not to see the creature's interest, but poured water from the jug into the eggshell until it was almost full. The creature in the cradle was seen to raise its eyebrows but again, the soldier pretended not to take any notice. Taking up the little spoon, he spooned a tiny quantity of malt into the eggshell and, as the creature

in the cradle watched fixedly, he took the shell to the fire
and began heating it at the edge of the embers.

"I can no longer keep quiet!" said the creature in
the cradle. "What are you doing, man?"

"Isn't it plain what I'm doing?" asked the soldier.
"Do you have to ask?"

"You're cooking in an eggshell!" said the creature
in the cradle.

"Oh, what rubbish," said the soldier. "Anyone can
see I'm brewing ale."

After a long silence, the creature said, "I am old,
ever so old. I have seen three forests grow and wither. I
have seen the seas run dry and fill. Yet I have never, in all
my long, long years, seen a soldier brew ale in an eggshell
before."

"Aha!" The soldier swung round on it. "You
ancient, ugly, wicked thing! You have given yourself away!
Now, in the name of God the Father, Christ the Son and
the Holy Ghost, be gone!"

He made a grab at it, but quicker than a snake, the
thing was out of the cradle and across the room. With a
hiss and a crackle, a flash of green flame, a hot, ashy smell
and a loud shriek, it vanished up the chimney.

A great sigh came from the lady, the lord and all
the others in the room, but the soldier turned to them and
said, "Now you must all leave. Now I must perform the
most secret and dangerous spells for the return of your
child. Go, please, quickly and no matter what noise you
hear or how long the silence may last, do not come in. If
you come in before the struggle is over, both the child and
I will be snatched away by dark powers." He shooed them
all to the door and repeated, as he closed the door on their
faces, "Whatever you hear, or do not hear, do not come
in."

As soon as the door was closed, the soldier took
up his cloak from the corner, unwrapped the child hidden
in it and placed the baby in the cradle. Then he banged on

the table with his hands; he shouted and stamped; he whistled and dragged chairs about the room. He clapped his hands and shouted magical-sounding words. Then he stood absolutely still, hugging himself and grinning, while keeping quiet. He kept quiet for so long that the people waiting anxiously outside the door sighed and moaned. When one put their hand on the door's latch, the soldier shouted so loudly that cries of fear came from the door's other side. The soldier gave a dreadful laugh, clattered the furniture, slammed cupboard doors, rattled the window-frames, walloped the pots on the hearth and screamed.

Then he opened the door. He drooped as he did so, mopped his brow and looked exhausted. "It was a desperate struggle," he said. "But I won."

The lord and lady and their servants rushed into the room, almost knocking the soldier over. They gathered round the cradle and the lady lifted the child in her arms. She smiled at the soldier.

"Name your reward!" she said.

"A castle," said the soldier. "Its treasuries to be filled with gold plate and coins and precious stones. Round the castle, a good forty square miles of farmland— an orchard— a carp-pond— and stock and servants, of course."

The lady, hugging her child, turned to her husband and said, "Give it to him!"

"Aah," said the lord, looking ill. "Well. My dear. I think I may have some trouble—"

"If that's too much," said the soldier, "I'll manage without the castle. Just give me the land and the treasure and I'll build my own castle."

"Give it to him!" said the lady. "He won our baby back. And you promised him whatever he asked for."

"Um," said the lord. "Yes, well. *Actually*—"

"All that would be a bit much for me to manage with my war-wounds," said the soldier. "War-wounds from fighting the war you sent me to. A small house would do, maybe. About the size of this small house. And, of course, the forty square miles, the orchard, the carp-pond, the stock and the servants."

"A house," said the lord. "But forty square miles…"

"A bit much for me to farm, I agree," said the soldier. "Say, twenty square miles— and forget the carp-pond. I've never liked fish."

"An orchard," said the lord. "Seven acres and a little house."

"Throw in the stock and it's a deal," said the soldier.

"Done," said the lord and they shook on it.

"I am your witness," said the lady. "I shall see that you are paid to the last square foot of land and the last apple-tree."

The soldier went happily home to his mother, sisters and brothers, having gained a far greater reward than the one he'd hoped for.

10

Blessing the Cliffs

In Iceland, along the fjords, there are steep cliffs where hundreds of seabirds build their nests on ledges and in little clefts in the rock. There they live, fish and raise chicks; and they fly and scream over the cliffs and the sea.

The people of Iceland used to lower themselves over the edges of these cliffs on ropes, to steal the eggs from the birds' nests— but trolls lived in the cliffs as well as birds. Too often a huge, grey hand, hung with shaggy fur, came out of the cliff's side and tweaked the ropes in two as if they were threads of cotton. Whoever was on the rope's end fell and was killed in the sea far below.

The habit of the trolls grew so bad that the people asked a Bishop to come and pray over the cliffs to exorcise the evil, heathen things that lived in them. The Bishop came in his heavy, brilliant, beautiful robes and, attended by others as stiffly and magnificently dressed as himself, he paced slowly along the cliff's edge, praying and sprinkling holy water while his attendants swung censors, carried candles and sang hymns. Again and again the Bishop called on the trolls, in God's name, to leave that place.

It took a long time but, at last, only one small stretch of the cliffs remained unblessed. Before the Bishop could reach it, a deep, thick, unhappy voice cried out, "Bishop! Bishop! The wicked do need somewhere to live."

The Bishop stopped short in astonishment— but then he said, "That is so." And he left that part of the cliffs unblessed and the trolls still live there. That's why it's called 'Heathen Cliff' and no one goes near it.

11

Dando and his Dogs

Once, in Cornwall, there lived a priest named Dando. He was not a good man. He thought that merely being a priest had saved his soul and therefore he had no reason to fear God. He drank, he smoked, he swore and he neglected his parish. He never visited any of his congregation except those that had pretty daughters or young wives and he preached only when the day promised poor hunting. He thought he'd done more than enough if, in crumpled vestments pulled on hurriedly, he rushed through a marriage service or christening and he'd been known to refuse to leave his house to give someone the last rites because it was raining.

The one thing that Dando was always keen to do was hunt. He led the hunt and his congregation knew that if the Sunday was fine, there was no point in going to church, for Dando would be out with his dogs.

An old woman once met him as he rode home on

Sunday evening with his kills hung from his saddle. "Dando," she said, "if you hunt on the Sabbath, you will be hunted."

Dando cared nothing for the opinion of an ignorant old woman who could not write her own name and the next Sunday he went hunting again, over the estate called Earth. The hunt had a long, hard chase and made several kills— for Dando would run down any animal that showed itself. Once or twice during the day he thought he noticed a stranger riding with them: a dark, quiet-faced man. But when he took a better look, he always found that he had been mistaken and the strange rider was, in fact, someone he knew well.

Late in the afternoon the hunt stopped beside a stream to rest the horses and to eat and drink themselves. Dando put his flask to his mouth and found that it was empty. He had drunk all his whisky in pauses during the chase. Turning to the man nearest him, he demanded a drink from his flask.

"Mine's empty too," said the man.

Dando turned to the man on his other side, but that man's flask was also empty. Dando shouted out that anyone who had any drink left was to bring it to him. But every member of the hunt had emptied their flasks.

"Get more!" Dando yelled. "I'm dry as a bone— I need a drink!"

"Dando, where are we to get it?" asked one of the other huntsmen. "There's not a house or a tavern for miles around."

"If none can be found on Earth," Dando shouted, "go to Hell for it!"

A man came up to where Dando sat on the stream's bank and held out a flask to him. Over the flask, the man looked intently at Dando with bright eyes, green as new grass. It was the man Dando had fancied he'd seen several times that morning. Now that he saw him plainly, Dando felt a coldness of fear come over him and his chitterlings crept within him.

"What's this?" Dando said, nodding at the flask.

"It's the finest drink 'stilled in the place you just mentioned," said the stranger.

Every other member of the hunt sat motionless and silent, but Dando laughed. "You won't frighten me with such talk, sir! I want drink and if it *does* come from Hell, I'll take it."

He snatched the flask from the stranger's hand, put it to his mouth and gulped down the drink it contained, to show that he wasn't afraid. The drink was the best he'd ever tasted and he took another drink, and another; and emptied the flask. He looked round boastfully— and blearily, for the drink had been strong. It was then he saw the dark, quiet man going from horse to horse, gathering together all the game that hung from the saddles. Everyone watched him, but no one seemed to have the courage to speak up.

Then the stranger went to Dando's horse and took Dando's share of the kill.

"What right have you?" Dando demanded, starting up from his seat beside the stream. He staggered over to the stranger and tried to snatch his kills back.

"This is the Sabbath," said the stranger. "Your kills are my due."

"Your due, damn it!" Dando shouted. "Return it at once, sir, or I'll see you in Hell!"

The stranger smiled. He shook his head and said, "What I have, I hold."

"Will you, by God, will you?" Dando lunged at the stranger, trying to grab him by the neck. "I'll have what's mine back if I have to follow you to Hell for it!"

The stranger sidestepped Dando easily and laughed out loud. He walked away from the priest, fastened all the game to his saddle-bow, and mounted his black horse. Still laughing, he kneed his horse towards Dando, seized him by the scruff of his jacket, lifted him from the ground and flung him across the saddle-bow too, as if Dando were nothing but a hare.

"What I have, I hold!" the stranger shouted. His black horse leaped forward so fast and high it might have been winged. It leaped straight into the middle of the stream but, instead of water being flung up, a rush of flame spurted into the air. It died down, leaving the water bubbling. Dando and the stranger were gone.

Dando never hunted the estate of Earth again, but someone did. Someone hunted there at night, in the deepest unlit darkness, riding hard and headlong over the rough ground, passing through hedges and woodlands as if they were air, hunting with a pack whose savage and continual baying held those who heard it paralysed with fear until the sound had died away, and then left them despairing.

No mortal could ride so recklessly in such darkness; no mortal ever owned such unearthly hounds and so it was said that Dando's ghost now led the ghostly hunt— but one or two people who had heard those hounds could not believe that Dando rode behind them. No, they said: he runs before.

12

The Troll Bride

Once, in Denmark, there was a young man who married a troll's daughter: a fine, strapping girl, much taller than him, with tremendous shoulders and forearms, a head of golden hair stiffer than gold wire, and a long, strong tail which she wagged when she saw him.

They married because they each felt perfectly suited to the other and they were happy together— but the people of the young man's village were not pleased. "What sort of marriage-service was that?" they said. "'Do you take this man?— Do you take this troll?' That can't be right."

Did you see how much the thing ate after the service?" others said. "Give it a week and it'll eat him."

Most often the villagers said, "What can he see in it?"

They were so suspicious of the troll bride that

none of them would have anything to do with her, even though she tried hard to be friendly. The village children, who had been told that she would eat them, threw stones at her, called her names and then ran from her in a panic. The women she spoke to turned their back on her and the men shied away from her as they might from a bear. They made her deeply unhappy.

Her husband appealed to his friends and neighbours to be kinder to her, but they refused. "You wait," they told him. "Wait until it shows its *real* nature." He went angrily back to his troll bride, swearing that he would have nothing more to do with his own people.

One Sunday, while the villagers were in church, the troll bride's father, a huge old troll with stiff black hair and a black beard, came to the barn where the newly married couple were living until the husband could build a house big enough for his wife. The old troll had travelled down from the mountains to visit his daughter and find out if she was happy. When he heard how the villagers were treating her, he scowled so that his brows covered his eyes. He showed his long teeth. He lashed his tail. To his daughter he said, "Will you throw or catch?"

"Oh Father," she said. "You won't hurt the poor little things?"

"Will you throw or catch?" repeated the big old troll, his hair bristling.

"I'll catch, Father," she said.

"Then come along," said the troll, and left the barn, his daughter and much smaller son-in-law following.

The troll led them up the hill to the churchyard where they waited, listening to the murmur of prayers and the singing of hymns from inside. The service ended and the people came out— and crowded back into the church at the sight an even bigger, fiercer and more frightening troll than the one they were already plagued with.

"Go round to the other side, daughter," said the troll and when she had gone to the other side of the church, he beckoned to the people inside. Some of them went out to him, too afraid to do anything obey; others were pushed out by the priest, who was afraid that the troll would destroy his church to reach them if he did not.

The troll picked the people up, one by one, and threw them over the church roof. They howled as they rushed upward and flapped their arms, trying to fly— but it was worse when they felt themselves begin to fall. Then their shrieks and moans were so comical that some of the villagers still on the ground couldn't help giggling. Until the troll picked them up.

On the other side of the church the troll's daughter caught them all as they came tumbling towards her, set them safely on their feet, straightened their clothes and patted their heads. When her father had thrown every one of them— except his son-in-law— over the roof, he came round the corner of the building and found them all standing, sitting or lying about his daughter's skirts, all of them shaking hard enough to shake off their clothes.

"If I ever again hear that you have made my daughter unhappy," said the troll, "we shall play this game *once* more. On that day, she will throw and I will catch. Do you understand me, people?"

All the villagers understood him very well and as soon as the troll had gone back to the mountains, everyone in the village called on the troll bride, to give her eggs and cakes and helpful hints. Everyone who met her wished her good morning and smiled, and the villagers soon discovered that, despite her fierce appearance, she was kind and gentle and eager to please.

They forget everything unkind they had said about her when she arrived and went about telling each other that they had thought from the first day that she was a 'lovely thing' and hadn't they always said the young village man had made a wonderful choice.

Before long the troll bride was gossiping with the neighbours every day, helping with embroidery and knitting in the evening and minding children. She was happier than she had ever been, but her husband, who hardly ever saw her any more, was somewhat bitter.

13

The Beginning of the Elves

In the days when Jesus was on earth, a woman lived in the north who had a great many children. She had so many that she was rather ashamed of them because she could never keep all of them equally clean and tidy or well-fed.

One day her neighbours told her that Jesus was around and about. He was coming their way and would probably stop to talk with them. The woman hurried home, called all her children together and did her best to see them all washed and all their heads of hair combed. She tried to find clean clothes for them all, to darn holes and sew on buttons, to let down hems or take them up, to inspect ears and necks and fingernails, to wipe noses and muddy knees and to say, "Stand up straight! Take your hands out of your pockets! Use your handkerchief! Stop scuffing your shoes! Don't fidget, don't pull faces, don't muss your hair!"

No matter how hard she tried, the children she wasn't washing and tidying at any one moment, ran away to play, and fell over and made their knees muddy and bloody, tore their clothes, fell in puddles, tangled their hair in trees and made themselves, in a dozen different ways, as untidy and grubby as they had been before she started.

So, when the poor woman, all hot and cross and panicky, glanced through a window and saw Jesus coming up her path, half of her children were clean and neat and the other half looked as if they had always run wild and had never had anyone to care for them. The woman was ashamed for Jesus to see them, in case He thought her a bad mother who did not try to look after her children. To all those children who had made themselves grubby again, she said, "Go out behind the house and hide. Don't let Him see you."

Off they went, thinking it a game, and the woman let Jesus in. She sat Him in the best seat and gave Him the best she had to eat and drink. Then she made her clean and tidy children stand in a row in front of Him.

"Woman, these are beautiful children," He said, "and much loved. But where are the others?"

"I have no others," she said.

"No?" said Jesus. "I was sure you had others."

"Only these," she said and smiled proudly at the row of neat, clean, well-dressed children in front of her.

Jesus was quiet as He looked at her. Then He shook His head and said, "Were you afraid of my judgement? Let those that are hidden remain hidden, for if they are not fit for me to see, they cannot be fit to be seen by anyone."

Then Jesus went away. The woman hurried out behind her house and called to the children who were hiding. She called all day, but they did not come. Thinking they were playing a joke on her; she went to look for them. She found their footprints where there was mud; she found grass trampled where they had played. She found fruit they had dropped on the ground, and toys they had thrown aside. But of them— nothing.

At Christ's command they had become the Hidden People— the *Huldrefolk*— the Elves. If they are ever seen, it is only for a moment and then uncertainly.

Their mother still searches for them, after all this time. Sometimes she comes where children are playing and goes from child to child, peering into their faces. Then she wanders away, calling, for the children she comes on are never her children.

14

"Isn't it Fun in the Dark?"

It was always the custom when a corpse was laid out, awaiting burial, for someone to sit beside the body with a candle burning, to keep watch.

If the body was that of a close friend or relative, the duty of watching was considered an honour and there were plenty of people willing to do it. But once, in Iceland, a man died who had no friends and no relatives who cared to admit the relationship.

In life, this man had been a powerful wizard, able to raise a thick fog by whirling a goat's skin round his head, call up the dead to question them and create monster by magic art which he could then send to attack people. Nor had he ever been a Christian, but had boasted openly, without fear, of his worship of the wicked old gods, Odin, Thor and Freyr. His body had been washed and laid out, but no one dared to sit beside it through the three long nights of the watch, even with a candle. But neither did they dare to leave the body of such a wicked man unattended.

The time for the watch to begin drew near and still no one had been found to do it. At last, several people of the neighbourhood went together to speak to a man named Hakon, who had gone viking in his youth and was known to be strong and courageous. They begged him to keep watch over the wizard's corpse.

Hakon liked the idea of the watch as little as everyone else, but he understood that someone had to do it. And he had been asked, so he agreed.

The first two nights of the watch passed by peacefully. The old wizard lay as still and as quiet as a corpse should. The candle-flame rocked gently to and fro on top of its tallow-column and Hakon smoked his pipe, hummed to himself and gradually became easier in his mind. Indeed, at the start of the third night's watch, he told his neighbours that he looked forward to the peace and quiet and was sorry that it would soon be over.

But that night, a little before dawn, the candle went out. In the sudden smoky darkness, before Hakon could move to make another light, the dead wizard beside him slowly sat up. The wizard turned his face towards Hakon, a pale blur in the night, and said, "Isn't it fun in the dark?"

Hakon gasped in horror, but knew that he had to think and act quickly. "Fun maybe," he said, "but not for you!" He grabbed the corpse by the shoulders and struggled to force it back down onto the table— but the corpse fought back and it was infernally strong. The rank breath it cast in Hakon's face made him faint and he felt his head reel and his knees weaken… Then the first real light of day shone through the window and onto the corpse's face.

"Oh, thank God!" said Hakon; and whether because of the naming of God, or because the daylight touched it, the corpse sank back on the table and moved no more.

The wizard was buried that day and a huge stone laid on his grave before nightfall, to prevent him from getting up again.

15

Kraka

Kraka was a giantess, a troll, who lived high in the mountains of Iceland, in a cave. She was strong and fierce and used to steal cows by picking them up and walking off with them. She ate these cows raw, cracking their bones between her teeth to reach the marrow.

She used to eat people too but only women and girls, never men. She liked men. She thought they were pretty. If she came on a pretty man, she would carry him home to her cave and keep him as a pet. It made her sad that these men never stayed for long, but always ran away at the first chance. She never gave up hope that one day, she would find a man who would stay. No young man with any looks was safe from her.

Not far from Kraka's cave there was a farm called Baldursheim and a young shepherd, named Jon, came there, looking for work. He didn't know the district and had never heard of Kraka.

The farmer took him on, even young Jon was very good looking. It turned out that Jon was an excellent shepherd, one that the farmer wanted to keep for a long time. He started to worry, though, as it was only a matter of time before Kraka noticed Jon. The farmer kept his thoughts to himself because Jon was an excellent shepherd and he didn't want to frighten him away.

As for Jon, he didn't know he was in any danger until the day he looked round to find Kraka behind him. She had crept up silently and was watching him. As soon as he saw her, before he could run or make a sound, she snatched him up and carried him off to her cave.

The cave was hard to reach and once he was set down, gently, on the cave floor, Jon saw that it was going to be difficult to escape. For a long time, it was impossible because Kraka stayed with him in the cave, crooning over him, stroking his hair and calling him by such names as, 'Tidbit' and 'Sweet Morsel.' He couldn't help noticing the bones which stuck up from the rubbish on the floor.

Soon Kraka grew worried that he wasn't eating. She put all kinds of troll treats and delicacies in front of him, but Jon wouldn't eat any of it, even though he was soon ravenous. He was afraid of what it might be. He'd also heard it said that if you eat a troll's food, you become a troll yourself.

After a couple of days, Jon started to look pale and thin. Kraka was afraid that her pretty pet might die. She begged him to eat and even tried to push food into his mouth, but he spat it out. At last, when he saw that this monster really cared about him, he said, "There's only one thing that could tempt me to eat."

"What is that, Honey?" Kraka asked.

"A twelve-year old shark," Jon said.

Kraka sat in silence and thought about that for a long time. She knew that the only place she'd be able to catch a twelve-year-old shark was a long way off, a good seventy miles of hard travel from her cave, at Siglunes in the far north.

She tried to persuade him to eat bone-bread; she tried him with blood-pudding, but he would not touch a single crumb— and that decided her to set out for the north, to fetch that shark.

Before she left, she told Jon several times that it would be best for him if he stayed where he was and didn't move, but finally, she left the cave and started for Siglunes. But she'd only jumped from one mountain to another a few times and had hardly covered twenty miles, before she became sure that Jon would have run away as soon as she'd turned her back. All the others had.

Back she went to her cave, at a run, and peeped in. Jon sat quietly on a boulder, where she'd left him, with his hands folded in his lap.

Kraka started out again, leaping from crag to crag and this time she went thirty-five miles before all her doubts and fears became too painful and she ran back to the cave. She crept up to it silently and peeked inside— and there was Jon, on his boulder, quietly waiting for her.

Then Kraka was happy. At last, she had found a man who loved her, despite her appearance and nasty habits. This time she ran and leaped all the seventy miles to Siglunes, wading fjords as she came on them, determined to catch a shark for her pretty little Jon.

She waded into the deep, cold sea and caught a shark as a boy catches a trout, tickling it and throwing it onto the shore. Taking it up, she ran all the way back.

What did Jon do, during his time alone in the cave? Well, he had guessed that Kraka would come back once or twice, to try and catch him out in his escape. He had seen her peep into the cave both times, though he'd pretended he hadn't. He'd seen the happiness light up her face the second time and he'd guessed that she really would go to Siglunes then.

He crawled to the mouth of the cave, keeping

Susan Price

hidden in cave Kraka looked back, and watched her go. As soon as she was out of sight, he started down the mountain, heading for the farm.

After his time in Kraka's cave, he was weak and unsteady on his feet, but the dread that Kraka might still come back and catch him kept him moving. He slid, slipped and clambered down the mountainside until he came in sight of Baldursheim.

Then he heard, behind him, the sound of heavy, crashing footsteps and Kraka's voice, yelling, "Jon, wait! I've got your shark— and it is a twelve-year-old— nearly a thirteen-year-old!"

Jon ran as hard as he could, despite his weakness. A sound of hammering reached him from the farm. As he got nearer, he saw the door of the smithy was open and the farmer was working inside. Jon ran across the farm-yard on wobbling legs, ran through the smithy door and behind the farmer, where he fainted.

The farmer was surprised and even more so when Kraka's great shape blocked the light from the smithy doorway. But the farmer had a cool head.

He had a lump of iron in his forge-fire, heated cherry-red. Grabbing it with tongs, he swung it towards Kraka, shouting, "Iron! Get out of here or I'll feed you this iron!"

Now one way to banish a troll or an elf is to show them iron. They cannot stand it. Kraka hastily backed from the forge door, not only because the iron glowed red-hot, but because it was iron.

The farmer followed her, brandishing the iron. "I charge you, in the name of God the Father, the Son and the Holy Ghost— and by this iron— never to bother me or my men again." Kraka, startled and thoroughly shocked by the iron, turned and ran away, taking the shark with her.

The farmer returned to his forge, put the iron back in the fire, and tipped cold water from his water-bath over Jon, to wake him up. Then he helped Jon inside, sat

74

him by the fire and gave him bread and cheese. Jon worked for the farmer for many years and married his daughter in the end.

Which goes to show that it pays to handle trolls firmly as well as men, since Kraka never did bother anyone belonging to Baldursheim again.

16

Michael Scott's Ride to Rome

In the days when Christendom was ruled from Rome by the Pope, there lived in Scotland a wizard named Michael Scott. He was a courteous, quiet man who attended church every Sunday but, because he dealt with devils and sorcery in his research, many said he was little better than a witch or a devil himself. The wizard ignored this gossip.

In those days only the Pope knew how to calculate the date of Shrove-tide, the day on which pancake days falls. Without knowing that date, it was impossible to calculate the date of Easter Day or Good Friday or Maundy Thursday or Palm Sunday. Each year, in every country of Christendom, a man was chosen to travel to Rome and learn, from the Pope's own mouth, the date of Shrove-tide. That man would bring this sacred knowledge home with him to his countrymen. In Scotland, one year, the man chosen was the wizard, Michael Scott.

But Michael Scott was busy with many other things, some of them having very little to do with Christianity. Days went by as he read his books and made his experiments— until he realized, suddenly, that it was Candlemas already, the last feast of the year, and he had not even thought about his journey to Rome.

Quickly, he pulled on a fur-lined gown with a hood and hurried outside into the dark and cold. With his staff he traced a pentangle in the deep snow. He stood inside the circle and spoke the incantation that would call up a demon. The thing appeared slowly, forming itself from the air, hating and angry but trapped by the pentangle.

"Were I to transform you into a horse," said the wizard, "how swift would you be?"

"Swift as the wind," said the demon, because the wizard's magic forced it to answer.

"Not swift enough," said the wizard and dismissed the demon to its own world. He spoke another invocation and another demon appeared.

"Were I to transform you into a horse, how swift would you be?"

"Swifter than the wind."

"You will not do," said Michael Scott. He dismissed that demon, called up another and asked it the same question.

"Faster than a sea-gale," said the third demon.

"Of use, but small use." And the wizard dismissed the third demon and summoned a fourth.

"As swift as thought," it said.

"Even you will hardly be swift enough," said the wizard. With another spell, he turned the fourth demon into a strange, ugly horse, and mounted it. Immediately, it leaped from the earth to the sky, whirling the snow into dense white clouds and leaving patches of black night showing through like holes in fabric.

They sped, faster than a breath, high above the land of Scotland, and of England and the demon said to its rider, "Tell me, Wizard, what do the old women say as they put the fire out at night?"

Michael Scott laughed. He knew that the demon was trying to trick him, for the old women said a prayer and if, in answer, he spoke the words of a Christian prayer to the demon, it would vanish and he would fall through miles of empty air to strike the earth below. So, he said only, "Ride on to Rome, demon and do not concern yourself with such matters."

In the space of blink, they passed high over the Alps, and the demon called out, "Come, Wizard, tell me: what do the mothers say when they put their sweet, sweet little ones to bed?"

The mothers spoke a blessing, so Michael Scott replied only, "On to Rome, demon and don't worry yourself about the mothers or their little ones."

A blink after that and they were in Rome. Michael Scott jumped from the demon's back and hurried into the Papal Palace, sending every guard he found running with the news that the messenger from Scotland had at last arrived. The Pope rose from his bed at once and came to see the Wizard— indeed, the Pope came so quickly that there was still a little snow on the Wizard's cap. But the Pope was angry and in no mood to be welcoming or helpful.

"You are late," he said.

"I was busy," said Michael Scott. "But now, at last, I am come."

"There is snow on your cap," said the Pope.

"It is the snow of Scotland," said Michael Scott. "It was snowing when I left."

"I do not believe you," said the Pope. "How can that be? There is some trickery here and I shall not tell you the date of Shrove-tide until you can prove to me that you have come from Scotland."

"I apologise," said Michael Scott. "I have fetched Your Holiness from your bed and you have had to dress in haste."

"In that, at least, you speak the truth," said the Pope.

"I know that I have," said Michael Scott, "because there is a shoe on your foot which is not your own."

The Pope looked down in surprise and saw, on his left foot, his own shoe— but on his right foot there was a pretty, pointed, embroidered yellow shoe.

Michael Scott said, "Wise men— and I am a wise man— do not ask how the Father of the Holy Church comes to have a woman's shoe upon his foot. I ask, Your Holiness, only to know the date of Shrove-tide."

There was a long silence while the Pope wondered how many cardinals and servants had overheard what the wizard had said. "Oh, very well," the Pope cried. "This year, Shrove-tide falls on the first of April."

"What?" said the wizard.

"The first of April!" shouted the Pope.

"Pardon?"

"The first of— Are you deaf?"

"No, Your Holiness, but I must be sure, because it's a long, dark, cold ride back to Scotland and I'm afraid I will forget the date on the way. Then I will have to come back and— get Your Holiness out of bed again. And who knows what shoes you might put on by mistake then?"

"The first Tuesday of the first moon of Spring is Shrove-tide," said the Pope, banging his hand on the arm of his chair. "Now there is no need for any more devil-dealing Scotsmen to come to my court!"

Michael Scott bowed himself out of the gracious presence, mounted his demon horse in the courtyard and, in a breath, flew back to the snows of Britain. As they flew high over the Pennines, the demon said, "Answer me one question, Wizard, if you can. What do women say when they cross themselves?"

"Never mind that, demon," said Michael Scott. "Fly straight before you, as I command, and forget about women, old, motherly or young."

He finished speaking just as the demon's hoofs struck the ground outside his house and, as soon as Michael Scott was off its back, the demon vanished, crying, "Good luck to you, Wizard, but curses on your teacher!"

And that was how Michael Scott brought back to Scotland not only the date of Shrove-tide but the secret of calculating that date, saving his countrymen the trouble and expense of sending a man to Rome every year.

17

The New Year Visitors

There were once two brothers who lived and worked a farm together. They often argued over whether there were such creatures as elves or not. The elder said that there were because he had seen them about the farmhouse at dusk. The younger said that there were not because he had never seen them and that any man who believed in such things was a fool.

This argument went on for years without either brother being able to feel that he had won, but at last it broke out in a quarrel so fierce that the younger brother said that he was unable to tolerate living with such a half-wit any longer and he was leaving. The elder brother was sorry for this, and asked him if he would not stay a day or two longer, to think things over.

"I will not stay another moment in this house with you!" said the younger brother, whose name was Peter.

"Oh, go on, then," said the older brother. "Go and find out what it's like, living on your own out in the world. I'll give it a couple of months before you come back here."

"On the day I find proof that the elves exist," said Peter, "that's the day I'll come back here." Which was his way of saying that he never would.

It didn't take Peter long to pack his belongings, which were few, and then he left home, taking with him the dog that had belonged to him since it had been a puppy. He earned his living by going from one farm to another and hiring himself out as a labourer. He also delivered packages and messages. It was a hard way of life, always walking the road, often sleeping in the open and going hungry but Peter was too proud to go back home.

One New Year's Eve, he came to a farmhouse he had never visited before and, to his surprise, found all the people of the house in a sullen, melancholy mood. Nothing had been done to prepare for celebrating the New Year. The house hadn't been decorated and no cakes had been baked.

The farm-people still invited Peter and his dog inside and gave them a place by the fire. They even gave them plenty of good, plain food, but none of them seemed to have heard of smiling.

Peter sat by the fire and ate his food in silence. No one else spoke. When he'd finished his meal, Peter dared to say that they all seemed very gloomy considering it was New Year's Eve.

"We all want to go to the midnight mass," said the farm-wife, "but we can't."

"Why not?" Peter asked.

"Because it's New Year," she said.

Peter waited, but she said nothing else. Her husband, seeing how puzzled Peter was, said, "We dare not leave the house empty, for fear of fire or theft. But we don't dare to leave anybody behind either because, when we did, we came home to find the house-minders dead. With all their bones broken."

"*All* their bones broken?" said Peter.

"All their bones broken. For three years running."

"Three years running!" said Peter.

"Each New Year's Eve for the past three years, we've left someone behind to mind the house while we went to Mass. And when we came home, the minder was dead, with all their bones broken. Something terrible has been visiting this house on that night. Maybe it won't come if we all stay home, but we dare not leave anyone alone here."

Peter sat quietly by the fire and he could not stop wondering what it was that visited the house on the last night of every old year. He looked around the old kitchen and saw that wooden panelling covered the walls. He got up and examined the panelling carefully. The farm people seemed too miserable to wonder what he was doing.

He took his seat by the fire again and said, "You can go off to your church-service, all of you, if you'll trust me to guard your house."

"What?" said the farmer. "You'll stay here alone, after what we've told you?"

"Yes," Peter said. "I'm very curious to see what it is that can break all the bones in a man's body. You've no need to be concerned. It's my own choice and I'm a stranger to you, so if I go the same way as the others, it will be no great sorrow to you."

Since this was true, and since everyone else wanted very much to go to church, Peter was able to quickly persuade them. They all put on coats, hats, boots and shawls and went out, leaving the house to him.

As soon as they'd gone, Peter jumped up and searched the house for tools, with his dog running excitedly after him from place to place. He searched hurriedly, for he could not tell when the thing that broke bones would come. He found a claw-hammer and a strong, broad-bladed chisel and, using these, he pried a part of the panelling loose and squeezed himself in behind it. He pulled the panelling roughly back into place and hoped he was well enough hidden. His dog ran about near the panelling, whining anxiously, but there was barely room in his hiding place for Peter, so he couldn't take his dog in with him. After a while, the dog lay down in the middle of the room, one eye fixed sadly on the spot where his master had disappeared. Peter made a hole in the panelling with the chisel, so he could peer into the room with one eye.

A few minutes after he'd made his peep-hole, he heard a chatter of voices and a crash as the farmhouse door was thrown open. Then there was a rush and rattle of many running feet on the kitchen's wooden floor. Peter put his eyes to the peep-hole and saw his poor dog snatched from his resting-place and thrown down so hard that every bone in his body might well be broken. Peter was so shocked and afraid that he shut his eyes tight and saw nothing more until he heard a voice say, "There's a terrible stink of human flesh about the place this time."

Peter opened one eye at that and looked through the peep-hole. He saw many little people, none of them more than four feet high, but so solid and strong in build and so ugly, fierce and malicious in appearance that they scared him. He wished heartily that he had never doubted the existence of elves, or volunteered to guard the farmhouse. The elves snuffed the air, snuffing his smell and soon they would find his hiding-place, drag him from it and break all his bones too.

But one of the elves said, "Why be surprised that the place stinks of human flesh when humans live here all the year round? And have left here a couple of eye-blinks ago?"

On hearing that the elves took deep breaths of relief and let them out with grunts and whistles. Their relief was nothing to that felt by the man hiding behind the panelling. He went on watching through his peep-hole. First of all, a young elf was sent to stand by the door, to keep watch.

Then the elves prepared for their feast. Some set about cooking in the farmhouse fireplace, unpacking large joints of meat. Others fetched in small barrels of drink.

Another party made the table ready. They pushed aside all the farmhouse furniture and set up, in the middle of the room, a table of their own. Over this they spread a beautiful white cloth with a thick, heavy hem of embroidery, worked in gold. They laid the table with bowls, plates, cups, jugs, spoons and knives, all of silver.

The smell of roasting meat made Peter's mouth water as he stood behind the panelling. He was hungry but he hoped that the smell of the food hid his own smell.

The elves came to the table and ate hungrily. Peter could hear them gobbling and slurping. Now and again they would bang on the table and yell. Peter wondered how long the feast would last and how long he had to stand there, behind the panelling, with aching legs and a hungry belly.

When they did, at last, finish eating, an elf at table shouted out to the young elf on watch by the door: "How goes the night?"

The young elf poked his head into the farmhouse and said, "Plenty of time yet."

The elves cleared the table and packed away all the silver tableware and the wonderful cloth. Then two of the elves, a man-elf and a woman-elf, stepped into the centre of the room and stood side by side. Another elf, a man-elf, stood in front of them and spoke some words before calling out again, "How goes the night?"

"Plenty of time yet!" the young elf called back.

The elves began to sing with a strange, high creeping noise which made all the hair on Peter's body stand on end and prickle. He clenched his teeth until the singing ended.

"How goes the night?"

"Plenty of time!"

The elves danced, stamping their feet, clapping their hands, shouting out songs and playing loud music on fiddles and drums. This went on for a long, long time, until Peter felt he must fall asleep where he stood, behind the panelling, for between standing and hunger and fear, he was exhausted. But at last, the dancing stopped and again there came the cry: "Door-keeper! How goes the night?"

The young elf looked in at the door and said, "Still one more watch."

Peter did not think he could stand this elf party any longer. Saying a prayer within himself, he took a deep breath and shouted as loudly as he could, "You lie! It's daylight already!"

The elves were startled— but they could only suppose it was one of themselves who had shouted. They panicked, because elves fear daylight, and they rushed about the room, scratching and chittering like rats, humming like bees.

One of the biggest elves seized the young door-keeper and shouted, "I'll teach you to mind your watch!" He threw the young elf down on the stone floor and broke all his bones. Pulling open the door, the elves all rushed out together, in a pack, shouting and screeching. They left all their belongings behind.

Peter pushed his way from behind the panelling and ran after the elves. He was just in time to see them, in the twilight of fading night, jump all together into a lake not far from the farmyard.

He ran back to the farmhouse, threw the body of the dead elf outside but picked up the body of his poor dog and wept over it. He laid the dog's little body in a corner and then tidied the room, pushing the furniture back into place. Everything that the elves had left behind, he gathered up and hid in another corner. Then he sat in the armchair by the fire, with the farmer's Bible in his hands, in case the elves decided to come back for their tablecloth and silver-ware.

Soon after, when it was light, the people of the farm came back from church. Finding Peter sitting comfortably by the fire in a tidy room, they asked if he had really kept watch all night.

"I did," said Peter, "and there was something to see." He told them everything that had happened and fetched out the treasure that the elves had left behind, and his poor dog, to show them. "I'm sorry, but I've damaged your panelling," he said.

"Never mind the panelling," said the farmer. "You've discovered what it is that visits us on New Year's Eve and I think that's worth a little chipped panelling." The farmer and his wife wanted Peter to take all the elvish treasure away with him, but Peter would not agree to this. He kept the wonderful, gold-embroidered table cloth for himself, since it would have been a pity to rip it in half, but the rest of the treasure he divided fairly between himself and the farmer. Even half the treasure was enough to make him a rich man.

Then he went home to his brother and told him that he would never again doubt the existence of elves or call his elders half-wits for believing in them. He didn't stay with his brother, though. With his half of the treasure, he bought his own farm and was a rich and lucky man until the day he died. It's also said that the elves never again visited the farm where he'd won his treasure.

18

Pan Twerdowski

Note: My Polish uncle told me this story, which he said was famous in Poland. He said that 'Pan' is a title, not a name and means something between 'master' and 'lord.' You can find out how to pronounce it on the internet, but it's said something like 'Pan tFairduvski.'

Four hundred years ago, in Poland, there lived a wizard, a nobleman who wasted his fortune on the study and practice of alchemy, witchcraft, medicine and astrology. His name was Pan Twerdowski.

He wanted to discover the Alchemist's stone, which would turn all base metal to pure gold; the Healer's stone, which would cure all disease; and the Elixir which would give him immortal life— for Twerdowski had so much to do, to learn, to discover, that above all things he feared that death would interrupt him. The older he grew, the stronger grew the fear until, at last, he decided to make a bargain for his life. Using his great knowledge of witchcraft, he marked out circles and pentagrams on the floor in salt. He lit braziers and threw bitter, stinking herbs into them; he cast a spell with a black knife, and he summoned the Devil from Hell.

Pan Twerdowski wanted immortality. The Devil wanted Twerdowski's soul. They spent hours in hard bargaining and finally it was agreed that Twerdowski should have twenty-four more years of life, that during all that time the Devil should perform any task Twerdowski ordered and answer any questions he asked; and that, at the end of that time, the Devil should collect Twerdowski, body and soul, and do with them as he pleased— but only if the soul and body were collected from Rome.

Twerdowski agreed, the Devil agreed; a contract was drawn up and Twerdowski signed it, in his own blood, with his longest finger. As soon as he completed the last letter of his name, he felt new strength come into his old body. He looked into a mirror. His hair was dark again, his face unlined and young.

"I am immortal," he said to himself. Oh, the Devil might think that he could claim Twerdowski after a mere twenty-four years, but Twerdowski was sure that, once those twenty-four years were ended, he would find some way to trick the Devil's into giving him another twenty-four— or even fifty. Now that he had his youth again, he was never going to give it up.

Young again, Twerdowski could work for hours, for days, in his laboratory, without tiring— and now he had the Devil's help in his research. Yet he made no progress. He discovered nothing more about the Alchemist's stone or the Healing stone. In fact, he rarely went to his laboratory or library any more.

Strangely, now he had youth and strength again, he lost interest in the sciences he had always loved. Instead, he had the Devil bring all the silver in Poland to one place and cover it over with sand, to hide it. Only Twerdowski knew where it was.

He demanded from the Devil the power to change

sand into gold by running it through his fingers; and so, he was vastly rich, with the power to buy anything or anyone. So, what did he care about science?

He took against a whole village because he fancied one man who lived there had insulted him. Because of that one man's insult, Twerdowski took a magnifying glass and held it above the name of the village on a map. The heat of the sun, shining through the glass, set fire to the map and burned the name of the village— and as the written name burned, so the real village burned to the ground.

In Krakov, the people were astonished and alarmed to see Twerdowski flying through the air above them on the back of a giant cockerel. The wizard looked down and laughed at them.

Instead of learning about the world, or helping people, Twerdowski passed the twenty-four years in gathering wealth for himself and playing silly or cruel tricks— and all the time, he grew not a day older.

Time kept passing, all the same and Twerdowski, waking one day, realized that he was in the twenty-fourth year of his bargain with the Devil; and now they were ending, they seemed not to have lasted twenty-four hours.

Twerdowski wondered if he was really clever enough to save himself from the Devil— and what had he gained that was worth selling himself into Hell?

"But my body and soul can only be collected from Rome," he told himself. Twerdowski had never been to Rome, and he had no intention of ever going anywhere near the place.

The day came that ended the twenty-four years. On that day, Twerdowski went for a long walk in the pine forests of his estate. He lay down beneath a tall pin tree, to rest and enjoy the forest and its scents for what might be the last time. As he lay there, clocks all over Poland turned their hands to the exact hour, minute and second on which, twenty-four years before, Twerdowski had signed the contract in his own blood. Less than a second after that, the Devil appeared, saying, "Where were you? I've been to Rome and you were not there."

"I was here," said Pan Twerdowski.

"Why were you not where you contracted to be, in Rome?" the Devil demanded.

"Because I do not mean to give up my soul or my body to you."

"You must go to Rome and you shall," said the Devil. "Order your coach. Send messengers ahead to open the frontiers and hire a ship— or climb on my back and I will carry you there in an eye's blink!"

"No," said Pan Twerdowski. "I shall not go to Rome with you, or alone, not with anything human or inhuman. I shall stay here and never die, for my soul is yours but you cannot have it."

"If you go not willingly, I shall punch and kick and whip you there!" said the Devil.

"Punch and kick and whip away," said Pan Twerdowski. "It cannot be as bad as Hell."

The Devil uprooted a pine-tree and beat Twerdowski with it, trying to drive him to Rome as an animal is driven, but though it was a terrible beating, though he was bruised all over and bleeding, Twerdowski would not move an inch but only cried, again and again, "It cannot be as bad as Hell!"

After a long, long time— days, weeks— even the Devil became exhausted and went away, wrapped in an angry storm. Twerdowski was so hurt, he could not move from where he lay and sobbed, "It was not as bad as Hell," into the pine-needles until some of his servants found him. He was so badly beaten, they hardly knew him, but carried him home and put him to bed. There he stayed for a year, recovering. Every moment, he expected the Devil to come to fetch him, but the Devil did not come.

Twerdowski began to think that he— alone of all humankind— had defeated the Devil. He flattered himself that no one in the world was cleverer than he was.

When, at last, he could rise from his bed, his bruises and wounds had healed, but he was a very old man. What sorcery he'd known, he'd forgotten. He found that his great horde of gold had turned back into sand. The silver the Devil had buried for him was still there, buried deep, and he could not reach it. (The silver is still there, in Olkust, and now it is mined.)

So Twerdowski had nothing left. He still remembered much of what he had learned of medicine and earned his living as a doctor. He soon became known as an excellent doctor and many rich lords and ladies came to him for treatment, even though they were a little afraid of him.

One day, the servant of another doctor came to him, with a message from his master. The other doctor was treating a very difficult case and needed advice. No one was more knowledgeable than the famous Pan Twerdowski. Would Twerdowski please come, urgently and give his advice?

Twerdowski was flattered by this compliment to his skill and he travelled many miles with the servant, in his master's coach.

On reaching the village, the servant led Twerdowski to the inn where the doctor was staying. He left Twerdowski to wait in the parlour while he went to fetch his master.

Twerdowski sat at a table and looked about him. On a bench close by lay a baby in a basket, kicking its feet and chuckling to itself.

From outside came a creaking noise as the inn's sign swung back and forth in the wind. It cast a shadow over the table-top.

There were other shadows too. Many ravens were gathering, scores and scores of them, perching on the inn-sign, on the inn-roof and on the buildings opposite. Their shadows fell across the table but they made not a sound.

A footstep made Twerdowski look up, and there

was the doctor who had sent for him. The doctor was dressed in a long black gown and wore a three-cornered hat. "Ah, Twerdowski," he said, and crossed the room with his hand held out to take Twerdowski's.

The old man stood, to shake the doctor's hand— but all the ravens croaked and screamed and flew about in a whirl of black wings.

Twerdowski took a sharper look at the doctor and saw the tip of a white horn poking through the three-cornered hat.

He looked up at the inn-sign that hung outside the window. The name of the inn was 'Rome.'

Twerdowski stooped and snatched up the baby, holding it in front of him.

The Devil had been about to seize him but now drew back. The baby was innocent and the Devil could not touch the innocent.

"Oh, Twerdowski," said the Devil-doctor. "'*Verbum nobile debet esse stabile.*'" (A nobleman never goes back on his word.)

Twerdowski was ashamed. He had willingly signed a contract with the Devil, but then had tried to go back on it, and to escape a debt which, eventually, he must pay. He had even been prepared to risk a baby's life rather than keep his word. In his eagerness to live forever, he had forgotten even his nobility. He put the baby back in its cradle— and the Devil snatched him up and carried him up through the roof.

Hordes of ravens flew into the air around them in a living, beating, screeching black cloud but the Devil and Twerdowski rushed upwards, beyond the birds, into air that was freezing cold. Looking down, Twerdowski saw the world shrinking, saw the villages becoming dots, saw the forests where he had walked, the fields, the hills, even Poland itself shrinking into pin-pricks and vanishing.

Twerdowski began to cry. He had loved his life on earth. As the world grew smaller still and all about him grew colder and emptier, his memory ran about among the things he had seen and done. Hardly knowing what he did, he began to sing a hymn he had learned as a small boy, a hymn in praise of the Virgin Mary.

His voice was strong and in the cold darkness it sounded sharp and clear. It was forced back to the earth by the speed of their ascent. The hymn echoed from earth's mountains and crossed valleys and the people in the towns and villages came out into the streets to listen. Farmers and shepherds, travelling-people and fishermen, all heard the singing and all listened, holding their breath and looking up into the black sky and at the white stars.

They were afraid and the hair prickled at the back of their necks, but it was a fear filled with beauty and longing. Many of them wept. "Whoever it is that sings has been wicked," they said, "but he repents and will be saved." As they listened, the song in the darkness brought them the certainty that they, too, would be saved and they were comforted.

Twerdowski, as he ended the hymn, was still in the Devil's grip. But a voice said, "Twerdowski, sinner though you are, you have cleansed My people's souls. Therefore, you shall not go to Hell— but neither can you return to the Earth. You must wait where you can for the Day of Judgement."

When this voice spoke, the Devil at once let go of Twerdowski and the wizard fell down and down the sky until, by luck, he landed on a horn of the crescent moon. There he sits still, waiting for Judgement and sometimes singing the hymns he remembers from his childhood. But these days, his voice is very seldom heard by anyone.

19

Lutey and the Mermaid

In the village of Curey, in Cornwall, there once lived a man named Lutey. He made his living, in the main, as a fisherman, although he grew vegetables in small garden beside his cottage and was not above taking useful things from a wrecked ship and coming home with oranges and lemons in his shirt, or rolling a cask of doubly-salted butter along the beach, or carrying a small keg of wine on his shoulder.

Sometimes he brought home a half-drowned sailor or ship's boy for although he was quick to profit from a wreck if he could, he was a kind man who always gave what help he could to anyone in trouble.

One day, after a bad storm, Lutey wandered the beach, looking to see if the storm had washed up anything worth bending down to pick up, since the sea was still too rough for him to go fishing. His little mongrel dog ran in circles around him, coming back whenever he saw his master stop, to sniff at what had been found. Lutey picked up a couple of coins, and some bottles which he could wash out and sell. Then, in a pool of sea-water caught among some rocks, he found a mermaid.

He stood looking at her for a long time, while his dog yapped from a safe distance. Lutey knew that she was a mermaid by the long, strong coiling tail, all silver and blue, which formed her body from the waist down. Above the waist... Well, she was more beautiful than the most beautiful woman Lutey had ever seen. His own wife had been pretty enough for anyone when he had married her but even combed, washed and dressed in her best, she had not looked like this creature. His wife's skin was brown and red, rough and weathered by wind and sun. The mermaid's skin was white, absolutely white, as white as the full moon on a clear night. And smooth, smooth as the satiny inside of a shell.

His wife's eyes and hair were dark brown, like his own. The mermaid's hair was almost as white as her skin but, as the wind lifted first one strand and then another, lights flickered through it: green and blue and yellow. Her eyes were large and grey—or blue. Or green.

Over the years, Lutey's wife had grown stocky and almost shapeless with keeping house for him and having his children. Lutey had known this would happen and he still loved her dearly— yet he could not look away from the mermaid's heart-breakingly slender arms and neck. He shook his head in astonishment and wonder. He hoped that he would never forget one line or colour of the sight before him.

The mermaid had been staring back at him while winding long strands of her hair around her fingers. Then she stretched out her beautiful arms to him and said, "The storm washed me up here, lad: wouldst carry me back?"

Lutey started at the sound of her voice, but then grinned through his beard. "Aye. I reckon I could carry a little thing like thee down to the water, even if be a mile out." He climbed down into the pool and lifted the mermaid in his arms. She put her arms about his neck, coiled her long tail round his waist and laid her head on his shoulder. "Parson wouldn't like this, could he see it," Lutey said. "But he can't and I shan't tell him." He lifted the mermaid from the pool and carried her over the long stretch of sand to the sea's edge. His little dog ran after him.

"Thou'rt a good man," said the mermaid, and rubbed her cold cheek against his beard. "If I could grant wishes and I said I would give thee three, what wouldst wish for?"

"That would take some studying," Lutey said.

"Study, then, lover," said the mermaid.

"Well…," said Lutey. "Well… There's a lot suffer from aches and pains, especially in this cold weather. I know my poor old gel does and it catches me sharp sometimes, in the back, when I bend… And then there's fevers and coughs and colds and all sorts. Aye, I reckon I'd wish for the power to heal if I was going to wish. That'd do some good for a lot of folk, that would."

"And second wish?"

"Well… Folk lose a lot of things and most of 'em baint got that much to lose. So, I'd wish next for the power to discover things lost. That'd be a help."

"And third wish, me lover?"

"Well… Them other wishes wouldn't be much use if they died with me. 'Cos I'm getting on. So, I'd wish that the powers could pass down to my sons and daughters. Aye, that I would."

He felt a coldness on his cheek as the mermaid kissed him. "Thou'rt a good man," she said. "As good as thou'rt handsome." And she kissed him three times more: on the eyelid, on the neck and on the lips. Kisses cold as sea-water.

"Hey, hey, hey," said Lutey. "Madam! I hope my

old gel baint looking this way. I got to go back to her, tha knowst."

The mermaid clung to him more tightly. "Come with me instead. Come with me, love. You sail over the water in your boats, you men. Hast never wondered what lies deep beneath? Deep, deep beneath?"

"I have wondered, often enough," said Lutey, "but I should drown."

"I wouldn't let thee drown, lad," said the mermaid. "I'd take thee where no man that breathes air has ever been; and I'd love thee."

Lutey reached the edge of the sea and waded into the cold water, carrying the mermaid to the deeper water where she could swim away. He shook his head. "I can't come."

The mermaid tightened her arms and tail about him with frightening strength. "Come with me, and be my love, Lutey. Come with me and see the sunken ships with their sails torn into rags and drifting with the tides; come and see their cargoes, all spilt, all spoiled. Come and search for coins in the sand down there, Lutey, my Handsome, come and dig for lost rings and broken necklaces, and for every precious stone thou finds, I'll give thee a kiss." And she kissed him again, with a touch even colder than before, a cold that struck him through and yet was strangely pleasant, exciting, thrilling. If he had wondered before what lay beneath the sea and its changing colours, now he wondered and longed to know ten times more.

"Why stay here, above the lovely water?" the mermaid asked, as she stroked his hair. "Why suffer the storms and the pains; why worry and work and run after every little thing that might put a crumb in thine mouth? We don't live so under the sea. We never worry about what might happen; we never worry about food. We have no needs. Let go, my love. Let go of your sorry world. Come with me. Sink with me into the darkness. Oh, come with me, Lutey, come with me, love; be my love, Sweet, come with me."

Lutey shivered as her cold kissed stole the strength from him and he sank to his knees in the sea, which rushed against his chest and splashed about the mermaid. He opened his mouth to say that he would go with her, when his little dog yapped and barked from the edge of the sea. The mermaid, startled, loosed her hold and Lutey turned his head.

Beyond the noisy little dog, he saw the beach he'd walked along that morning; and beyond the beach he saw the small, poor cottage where he lived. He saw smoke rising from the holes in the roof; he saw his wife in the vegetable garden, stooping to pull something up; and he saw three of his children running, one after another, onto the sand.

Lutey knew then that he could not go with the mermaid; and he felt such painful sorrow for that— and for the dwindling, wasted life of his wife, and for the lives of his children which were yet to waste, that he felt a long sharp knife had been driven into him. Tears came to his eyes.

"Oh, Sea-maid, I would come— I would come— but look. Dost see my old gel back there? My poor old gel. If I go with thee, who's to dig the garden for her when her back aches and get the vegetables in for next year? See the holes in the roof? Who'd mend 'em? See the smoke? Who'd chop wood for the fire? Who'd find the money to feed and clothe the little uns if I wasn't here? My old gel, she'd try, but she's too old now to work so hard alone, and too old to do any better than me. I've got to stay and look after her and them— and have them look after me."

The mermaid wrapped her arms tightly round his neck, lashed out with her tail and dragged him beneath the water. But Lutey was a strong man and the water was yet shallow. He struggled and brought his head into the air again; and he dragged his knife from his belt and held it before the mermaid's face, knowing that all such creatures are afraid of cold iron. He said, "Go, in God's name!"

The water was thrashed into foam all around him as the mermaid swam away. At a distance she rose from the water again and called, "Thou'rt a good man, Lutey, and each one of thy three wishes shall be granted. I prophesy, too, that neither thee nor any of thy children, nor thy children's children, nor any born of thy line shall ever, from this day, be hungry or cold. But thou art mine, Lutey, and I shall have thee. I grant thee nine more years to live in the air and then I shall come and fetch thee home, lad." She sank beneath the water and Lutey waded back from the sea to his family.

Within a few days he had a chance to test the truth of the mermaid's words, for his youngest child fell sick and could not sleep; but after Lutey stroked her head and kissed her, she slept deeply and woke cured.

Word soon spread from house to house that Lutey of Curey could heal. People began coming to him when they were in pain, or feverish, or had wounds turning bad, or sores or coughing-fits. Lutey's touch and skill always brought ease. When it became known that he could also find things that were lost, still more people came to him. They all brought payment in eggs, or cake, or milk, or cheese and sometimes even in money. The mermaid had spoken truly when she'd said that Lutey's children would never again be cold or hungry.

On the ninth anniversary of the day he'd found the mermaid, Lutey went fishing with one of his youngest sons, a boy barely eight years old who already possessed some of his father's powers. They fished all day, made a good catch and, as the light faded, were thinking of putting back to shore. That was when the mermaid rose from the water near the boat, stretched out her lovely arms and called Lutey's name.

Lutey stood and made as if to jump overboard. His son, frightened, clutched at his father's legs. Lutey looked down at him and said, "I stayed then. Now let me go." Bewildered, the boy let him go and Lutey threw himself into the sea. He sank and did not rise, for the mermaid took him down with her.

Lutey's son was left alone in the still rocking boat as the air grew cold and dark over the sea. He rowed home alone without his father and no trace of Lutey was ever seen after that. Neither his body, nor his clothes nor anything belonging to him was ever washed up for mortals to find.

Lutey's son grew and came into all the powers the mermaid had granted his father. He had second sight too: the power of seeing the future. Some said that after he'd seen the mermaid take his father, the boy always looked so hard for what was not to be seen that at last he saw its shadows— moving shadows at the corners and edges of rooms, shadows among the trees and stone field-walls of the land and shadows among the rocks of the beach. Shadows miming what was yet to happen.

But he never lived to have children, this second-sighted Lutey. He still followed his father's trade of fisherman and, nine years after his father jumped into the sea, the young man went fishing with his younger brother. The mermaid rose from the water beside the boat and called to him. Without a word, without hesitation, Young Lutey swung himself over the boat's side into her arms and sank with her into the deep, cold sea.

His brother lived to marry and *his* children inherited the family's gifts, as did their children and their children's children. Indeed, for many generations there were no healers in Cornwall so famous as the Luteys of Curey; but every nine years the mermaid rose from the sea and called for her payment; and another Lutey drowned.

More Books by Susan Price

Crack a Story

A red squirrel...
A stone squirrel...
a stone squirrel of red carnelian runs up and down a
tree, cracking nuts.
For every nut the squirrel cracks, she must tell a
story.
Gold nuts, glass nuts, nuts of paper, nuts of
copper...
When the poison nut is cracked, what story is let
loose?
Tales of love...
Tales of adventure...
Tales of danger and magic...
Which nut will you crack?
Which story will you hear?

A beautiful collection of retold folk-tales featuring
bold, brave heroines.

Susan Price is an acclaimed writer for young
people. She has won many awards, including the
prestigious Carnegie medal and the Guardian prize.

The Story Collector

"I'll see you home," said the dog.

Old Mr. Grimsby collects stories as a hobby. He writes down stories told by his maid and by her grandmother, Mrs Naylor. He listens to stories at the bedside of the dying Mrs. Riley.

A hero of Waterloo, Sergeant Lamb, tells him stories if paid with pairs of old trousers.

Because everybody has a story.

Walking home one night, Mr. Grimsby finds the Churchyard Grim at his side, the ghostly dog that guards the graveyard and is dead.

The Grim tells a story as it leads him to Heaven's Gate. There he finds Sergeant Lamb waiting for the gate to open, and the Sergeant tells another story to pass the time.

Once inside, there's Mother Mary and She has a story to tell too.

Everybody has a story.

If you like the old stories, the wise, haunting, poetic, funny old stories passed down for centuries, then you'll love Susan Price's tales within tales, of the stories and the people who told them.

Head and Tales

It's 1770 and Linnet lies dying beside the 'stinking ditch' he has helped to dig for miles.

His last desperate wish is for his children to go home to his mother, whom they have never seen. But how are they to reach her safely, without money or knowing the way?

He begs his work-mates to cut off his head so the children can carry it with them. Fever-talk, plainly, but still... A promise to a dying mate is a serious thing. So, when the children start their long walk, they carry their father's head with them, wrapped in his old work-shirt.

But what use is a dead man's head when the children meet danger and difficulty?

Then the head opens its eyes and tells stories.

Stories have power.

Almost as much power as a father's love.

ABOUT THE AUTHOR

Susan Price has won the Carnegie medal and the Guardian prize and her many books have been sold around the world. She has a life-long love of folk-tale and legend and has published several collections of retellings.

Among her other books are:

The Sterkarm Handshake
The Ghost Drum
The Wolf's Footprint

Her website can be found at:

https://www.susanpriceauthor.com/

7:30

- 6:30

01494

862 855

463 899

Tuesday

07 9392 11260

0868 806

07854
875 246